The Edge of the World

'There ain't no such things as ghosts,' said Wilf Piggins. But Kit Huntley and pugnacious Tekker Begdale know better. They saw a ghost behind old Ma Grist's house at the end of Mr Huntley's orchard – a creature with a horse's skull. Between them they stumble into a strange and terrifying desert land and, unintentionally, involve Kit's infuriating and disbelieving brother Dan, whose life becomes endangered.

Enemies, fear and awe lurk around every corner as Tekker and Kit search for the one person in that desert land who can save Dan's life.

JOHN GORDON

The Edge of the World

Fontana Lions

First published in Great Britain 1983
by Patrick Hardy Books: The Archon Press Limited
First published in Fontana Lions 1985
by William Collins Sons & Co Ltd
8 Grafton Street, London W1

Copyright © 1983 by John Gordon

Printed in Great Britain
by William Collins Sons & Co Ltd, Glasgow

Contents

For Sylvia
from the first

1

The Betrayal

'There ain't no such thing as ghosts.' Wilf Piggins shifted his bulk against the parapet of the bridge and waited for someone to contradict him. Nobody did. 'And anybody who reckon he's seen one is mad.'

That's me. Kit Huntley leant over the parapet in the twilight and watched the dim reflection of her hair swing in the water. I've seen a ghost. But Wilf will never know.

'Old women,' said Wilf. 'It's always old women who see things.'

Kit tried hard not to laugh. Tekker Begdale had been with her when they saw the ghost – the ghost-like thing – and he wasn't an old woman. She willed her mind down to where he lay near the water's edge and tried to make him look up at her and laugh. This time he did not feel her glance, although he sometimes did. He lay with his hands under his ginger head and gazed up at the stars.

'So anybody,' said Wilf, 'who reckon he's seen a ghost is an old woman.'

Idiot. Big, fat, boring idiot. Oh, I wish I could tell him. But it's a secret. Just Tekker and me. She watched Wilf scrub his knuckles along the stone parapet. Big and tough; that was his style.

'Ain't it gone quiet?' he said. He sounded satisfied. 'Don't nobody want to tell us about ghosts they seen?' He paused, then shrugged. 'I reckon all the old women have gone home. Bed-time.'

Kit looked at the others leaning or sitting on the wooden railings along the bank leading up to the bridge. Wilf was right; they would soon have to be going. Nobody was going to quarrel with him; not so late on a summer evening. Not in the holidays.

Then a girl giggled from somewhere near the water's edge.

'Somethin' funny?' said Wilf.

'Only if you know what I know.' It was Betty Sutton, sitting on the grass alongside Tekker. She had a wide, soft mouth and a braying voice.

'Tell us,' Wilf ordered. 'I could do with a laugh.'

'Daren't. Not after what you just said. It's about a ghost.'

'That don't matter. We all know you're an old woman.'

'Then that's where you got it all wrong, Wilf Piggins. The ghost ain't nothin' to do with me.'

'Some other old woman, then,' said Wilf.

'Nothin' to do with you who it is.' She turned her back on him.

'You got a big mouth, Betty Sutton. You ought to keep it shut.'

That hurt her, and she bowed her head. Tekker stretched out his legs, and Kit watched him. Everybody watched him.

'You don't have to worry about what he says, Betty.' He yawned. 'We all know Wilf.'

'What you say, Begdale?' Wilf lurched forward.

Tekker raised himself on one elbow. 'Talking to me, Wilf? Finished bullying the girls?'

'Watch it, Begdale.'

Tekker sat with his elbows on his knees, his head

turned away as though he, too, knew he had gone too far. Wilf grunted and shifted his weight, still top dog.

Then Tekker said, 'It was me who saw the ghost, Wilf. I told her.'

There was a shout of laughter from Wilf and his hangers-on, but Kit barely heard it. She was pushing through them, her eyes blurred already with tears and anger. Tekker had told Betty. He had told her. All about the ghost. And it was a secret. Just us two.

'What's up with her?' said a voice.

'Seen a ghost, I reckon,' said Wilf.

Laughter welled up from the gallery along the railing and she ran, wanting to put it behind, but somebody stepped in front of her and held her shoulder.

'Let me go!'

'No.' It was Dan, her brother, two years older and much stronger. 'I want to see what happens.'

'I don't!'

'Young Tekker's bitten off more than he can chew this time.' Dan's glasses glinted against his long face.

'I don't care! He deserves it!'

She struggled, but Dan had a painful grip on her elbow. He was fifteen, raw-boned and tall, more than a year older than Tekker but friendly towards him. Tekker's wildness amused him.

'I don't want to see that kid get in too deep,' he said.

'Let him!'

Then one of Wilf's group broke in. It was thin Lenny Granger. 'Yeah, let him.' He could not have heard everything they said from the bridge, but enough. 'Let Ginger Begdale alone. He's seen a ghost. Ain't it enough?' There was a laugh, and Lenny turned to his master. 'He's just an old woman, ain't that right, Wilf?'

It was then that Tekker moved. Fast. He was up the

bank and over the railing to stand at the end of the bridge before another word was said.

'What did you say, Lenny?'

Kit watched him. His redhead's skin was always pale, but now its whiteness made his eyes flare like a madman's.

'What about it, Lenny? You going to stand there all night?'

There was a pause. Lenny was half behind Piggins. Nothing was going to make him come out.

Dan moved forward. 'Come on, Tekker.' The round head with its tight red curls swung his way. 'You've done enough. Let's go.'

Piggins stood clear of the parapet. 'What's this got to do with you, Huntley?'

'About as much as it's got to do with you, Piggins.'

They were face to face. Both older than Tekker, both taller. Piggins had the weight, but Dan, in spite of his glasses, had a bony strength, and Piggins knew it. Dan had raised one hand to unhook the wire frame of his glasses, when Tekker stepped in front, into range.

'Hey, Wilf,' he said. 'It's me who started all this.'

'Get out o' the way.'

'Not until you prove you ain't scared.'

'Scared? Who's scared of you?'

'I know what scares you.' Tekker stood with his hands at his side, on the brink of disaster. 'And so does everybody else. It's obvious.'

From the folds of his face, Wilf's little eyes, hot as needles, watched and waited.

'Ghosts,' said Tekker. 'You're scared of ghosts, Wilf.'

A split second of silence and Wilf's laughter exploded. He even put an arm around Lenny's shoulder.

'When you're finished.' Tekker waited. Wilf turned his laughter off. 'I somehow don't think you dare go to where I saw that ghost.'

'Any time, Begdale.' He moved forward, his arm still around Lenny. 'Just you lead the way, son.'

'Oh no.' Tekker did not stir. 'Not everybody. You've got to leave your bodyguard behind.'

'Anything you like.' Wilf pushed Lenny aside. 'Lead the way.'

Still Tekker did not move. 'I wasn't thinking of going right now.'

An oily grin curved Wilf's flesh. 'Called your bluff, did I, Begdale?'

'Not yet.' Tekker's voice was very calm. 'You can try that at midnight.'

'What you mean?'

'I mean midnight. Tonight. Just you and me.'

'That's a get-out, Begdale.' Wilf was sneering. 'You got to be home at that time. Tucked up with your teddy bear.'

'I can make it.' Tekker's voice remained level. His gaze was steady on Wilf. 'Can you?'

'Where's this ghost supposed to be, then?' Wilf was beginning to bluster.

'You'll find out.' Tekker was already turning away. 'If you turn up. See you here. Midnight.'

He was walking away before anybody spoke, and when voices were raised he kept on going.

Dan was catching him up. Kit trailed behind.

'Hey, young Begdale. What's all this about.'

'Not so much of the young Begdale.'

They were well clear of the bridge and following the curve of the churchyard wall under the trees. Tekker had slowed and they came alongside.

'What have you two kids been up to?' said Dan. 'And I want to know what's been going on.'

'Ask him.' Kit was savage. 'He'll tell anybody. Even Betty Sutton.'

'So what's wrong with Betty?' Dan, much taller than

his sister, was very different. Even his hair was fair, where hers was dark. And her face was round in contrast to his high cheekbones and thin mouth. 'I quite like Betty.'

'So does he! Those horrible gooey eyes and that great big squashy mouth that's always talking. Always!'

'About ghosts,' said Dan, 'the last I heard.'

'Ask him,' she repeated. 'It was a secret, but that don't matter to him!'

'Doesn't.' Even now, Dan corrected her and turned to Tekker. 'You've been leading my little sister astray again, have you, Begdale?' he said, but he was amused. 'Last week it was mind-reading, now it's ghosts.'

'Mind-reading worked,' said Tekker. 'We really were making it work, weren't we, Kit?'

'Don't talk to me.' She turned her back, but spun suddenly in a flare of skirts and spoke to Dan. 'Ask him about Ma Grist's cottage. Ask him about that.'

Even in the twilight and the dimness under the trees they saw Dan's face stiffen. 'You haven't been there, have you?'

His voice was so icy that for a moment it silenced Kit, but Tekker said, 'It was my fault. I know your father doesn't like us going down there.'

'Down there' was the far end of their father's orchard. He was a fruit-grower and one of his orchards stretched away behind their house to where old Ma Grist lived alone.

'There's been trouble with her before,' said Dan. 'You'll get in a hell of a row if my father finds out you've been disturbing her.'

'Keep your cool,' said Tekker. 'She didn't see us. All we did was peep through the hedge.'

'And saw a ghost!' Dan's voice was full of contempt. 'Did you know my father was trying to pacify her? He wants to buy her land.'

Kit saw Dan's anger and tried to smooth it. 'But she didn't see us, Dan. Really.'

'All you saw was a ghost, I suppose.' He saw their mouths open, but he refused to let them speak. 'If you're mad enough to go anywhere near there tonight, young Begdale, you'd better steer well clear of my father's orchard. Come on.'

He tugged at Kit, and they left Tekker standing by the wall picking at the cement between the bricks and wondering what he had to do to please anybody.

2

.

Creature in the Reeds

Kit got out of bed and crossed the room to the window.
The land was flat for miles, and the house rode like a ship
on a black ocean. The night was warm and there was no
moon, but half a mile away she could see the church tower
in the dark island of trees that marked the village.

Tekker was somewhere there. She screwed up her eyes
as though she could pick out his hidden house. It was
small, one of a terrace squeezed along the roadside by the
river, and always she felt cramped inside it. He was mad.
He'd never get out without waking somebody.

*

Tekker had not gone to bed. He sat by his bedroom
window in the darkness, listening to the house and
waiting for his chance. His father was long since home
from the pub, but was still downstairs, working at his
desk in the corner of the room below. The doors were open
and he heard papers turn over. It couldn't be long now.
His father had to be out early among the orchards where
he was a fruit agent, buying and selling.

Tekker raised his eyes from the narrow gardens behind
the houses. Far out across the fens a car's lights twinkled
through a row of trees and vanished. Zap, and gone. Like
a shooting star. He grinned and let a thought shoot with
it. Towards Kit, fast asleep. You don't need to worry

about Betty. I didn't tell her much. Only enough to give her a fright. She frightens easy. He hummed and stepped up the power of the thought, letting it roll away across the flat land to Kit's house. Dan was right; they had tried sending thoughts to each other. It might reach her, in her sleep.

*

Kit caught a glimpse of her room in the dressing-table mirror and shivered. The high ceiling hung overhead like the roof of a cave, and she, in her nightdress, drifted beneath it like something pale and dead. She shivered again. I wish I hadn't been so angry. I know he only told Betty to frighten her. She turned back towards the window and let the thought flicker outwards briefly. It might reach him. No, it was useless. Reading thoughts had never worked, no matter what he pretended. Such things never did.

*

Tekker felt warmth drift in through the open window. He sighed. Thought-reading was pretty useless. Then, from the room below, papers shuffled for the last time and a light clicked off. Time to go, Kit. Any minute now.

*

She heard the church clock begin to chime the quarters. Time to go. The cold bell-tune was almost drowned by the dark trees, but still she had to stiffen to prevent a shudder as she put on her clothes. I know he's going through the orchard in spite of Dan. You won't know it till you see me, Tekker Begdale, but I'm coming with you.

*

I wish Kit was with me. Fatty Piggins is no use. He'll

never see a ghost, even if it comes – which it won't; not
with him around. Too much like Dan, even though they
hate each other. Won't believe a thing unless they can
touch it. Spoil everything.

Tekker listened hard. For a big man, carrying a lot of
weight, his father moved very easily. His footfalls could
barely be heard as he climbed the stairs, but then he was
at the top and in the bathroom.

Just in case, Tekker thrust his pillow and a bundled
shirt under the sheets to make a sleeping hump, and then
he was out of the room and the door was shut behind him.
His father's weight had ironed the creaks out of the stairs
and he went down without a sound. Not that it mattered.
His mother had been in bed more than an hour, and now
the washbasin tap upstairs made the pipes rattle to cover
him as he crossed the kitchen and found his shoes. Their
soft soles squeaked once on the tiles until he remembered
to slide forward slowly. Then the key turned almost
silently in the lock and he was outside, taking a warm
bubble of house air with him.

Once before he had crept out of the house when
everybody was asleep, but then he had gone only to the
bottom of the garden and stayed until a cat came and
stared him out. This was different. He was a night
traveller.

A narrow tunnel penetrated the row of dark houses,
and he went through it to the road at the front. Across the
road, the river lay flat and still between grass banks, and
beyond it more dark houses lined the way to the centre of
the village. Like a horse, Tekker could spread his nostrils.
He sniffed the night.

*

Kit had a torch. She did not dare risk the orchard without it. She would wait there until Tekker came, just in

case her father should see him and think he was a
burglar.

*

He stepped out from the tunnel. The tiny crunch of grit
under his feet seemed loud, but he walked away quickly.
Soon he was running, keeping his footfalls soft. He was
late.

*

She moved slowly towards the long rows of dark trees
that came almost to the back door. She paused at the
entrance to the gloom under the branches and listened.
I'm late. They're already in there, by Ma Grist's hedge.
She entered the dark avenue.

*

He felt the night air whisper in his ears as he ran. He
could see the bridge. But no Wilf. Then a car's headlights
swept over it and he paused in case it should come along
the river towards him, but it went into the road between
the baker's shop and the Five Bells and throttled away
into the distance. It was then that a figure came from
behind a telegraph pole, showed briefly under the solitary
street lamp by the bridge and vanished.

He found Wilf around the corner, deep in the porch of
the public hall.

'Where have you been, Begdale? I been standin' here
hours.' He was jumpy and angry.

'Keep your voice down.'

'Why should I?'

'Please yourself.' Tekker grimaced in the shadow of the
porch. Wilf was going to be a problem.

'Let's get going then.' Wilf began to move out. 'I ain't
spending all night in the churchyard.'

'Who said churchyard?' Tekker had not budged.
'We're going to Ma Grist's.'

'Wha'!' Wilf spun round. 'You never said nothing about that, Begdale.' The thought did not appeal to him, and he began to back down. 'That's a mile away.'

'Not if you take a short cut through Dan Huntley's orchard.'

'I ain't going through no orchards.'

'All right, we'll go the long way.'

'I thought we was going to the churchyard. That's what I come out for.'

Tekker said nothing. He left it to Wilf, and he saw him hesitate, doubts churning. Wilf wanted to go home, but he was afraid of what the others would say, and suddenly he was on the move.

'I got to get some sleep tonight, Begdale. Let's get there. Ain't you ever going to start?'

They stepped from the shelter of the porch. No cars had gone by as they talked, and every last bedroom light in the village had gone out. It was the silence that made Wilf keep his voice low.

'I reckon it's getting cold,' he said, but the night was warm.

*

A leaf trickled along Kit's bare arm and she shivered. The low branches all bent towards her, heaping deep shadows.

*

They left the bridge behind them and moved quickly past the Rectory garden, where shadows seeped into the shrubs. Soon the last houses were behind them and they were moving out over the flat land with the sky wide overhead. Tekker sucked in the night air. He wanted to run.

'Lot of stars,' he said. 'You can almost see by them.'

'It's the only light we got.'

'Don't worry, Wilf. It's enough.'

Wilf grunted.

Tekker rocked his head and the stars seemed to flare, pricking the water in the ditches alongside the road with points of light. Wish I wasn't with this big fat nit. He doesn't see a thing, Kit. Nothing.

*

She stumbled in the dry, ploughed earth under the trees. She could see nothing; just a broken trench of stars between the leaves overhead.

She forced herself to stand still and listen. Curtains and folds of darkness hemmed her in and thickened the silence. Not a leaf stirred. But Tekker could not be far away.

She shielded her torch and switched it on. A thin beam escaped between her fingers and reached along the avenue of grey trunks but was swallowed in blackness before it showed the last of them.

'Tekker!'

Even her whisper was swallowed. She switched off the light and listened to herself breathing. She hated him.

*

He stopped where the road curved away, and a track forked from it to plunge between dark orchards. He noticed that Wilf kept close.

'Not far now,' he said. Somewhere away to their left would be Kit's house beyond the outskirts of the village but hidden by the endless sea of trees. And ahead, set back from the track, should be Ma Grist's cottage. He crouched to get a better view of the skyline. 'I can see her chimney,' he said.

'Keep your voice down,' said Wilf.

*

In the tunnel of the orchard trees, Kit sensed the black wall of the hedge ahead. Beyond it was the cottage, and Tekker must be close. She stood still, listening.

*

Tekker paused. Tall reeds in the dykes along the path were more than head height but he saw a gap.

'It's through there,' he whispered.

They went forward silently on the dusty track.

*

Kit came up to the thick hawthorn and held her breath. Where was he?

*

A plank bridge lay across the dyke.

'We done what we said, Begdale. We gone far enough.' Wilf's whisper was breathless.

'Not yet.' Tekker moved forward. 'We've got to wait for the ghost.'

'Don't be bloody stupid, Begdale! There ain't no ghost!'

'I'd like to see.' He stepped onto the planks between the tall reeds.

*

Kit crouched. Through the hedge roots she could see the cottage.

*

The cottage loomed ahead. He took another step onto the bridge and heard Wilf scuffle in the track behind him.

It was then that it happened. Across the waste ground of the derelict garden, he saw the cottage door swing inwards.

He jarred to a standstill. Behind the hedge, a jolt of panic froze Kit's crouch.

Very slowly, the black opening of the doorway filled, and Ma Grist stood there. She was short and stout. She wore a dingy-pale wrap-around apron, and her round face was solid and grey in the thin light.

He stood stockstill. His only chance was to be a shadow in the reeds.

Then her rimless glasses gave off a single dull glint directly at him, and she raised one of her thick arms and beckoned. He felt the pull, but fought it. Then the little mouth between the grey cheeks opened and a sound came from it. Not a voice. It was a bird-like chirruping, thin and whickering, as though her mouth was full of tiny, squeaking creatures and she was letting them out to pierce and bite and poison the air.

The sound roughened Kit's skin. Birds. She forced herself to believe it. Birds disturbed at their roosts. Tekker must be there, on the other side.

She strained to peer through the hedge and saw Ma Grist. The old woman had her back towards her. Kit saw the tight bun at the back of her head, and the raised arm. And beyond her, the wall of the reeds in the dyke.

The sound ceased, but alongside him Tekker heard the reeds stir. Near him something was moving. Something huge. The twittering came again, raking his skin.

Kit saw it. A shape parted the reeds. The ghost.

She was pushing herself back on all fours when it showed itself. A long, pale head, like a horse. It was grey in the starlight and its eyes were black sockets. It swayed, but before its shoulders pushed clear she was thrusting and stumbling backwards.

Tekker, ten paces from it, saw the head dip. A horse. Only a horse. It had never been anything else. A horse. Not a ghost.

Then it stepped out. Grey head on a black neck, and its mane cropped to a stubble. A horse. But walking on two legs. Its feet prodded the ground and its forelegs hung like arms.

He heard a scuffle behind him and Wilf had gone. He backed away as the bristled crest above the long head swayed towards the woman. It began to circle her on jerking, prodding legs, and he saw its face. It was as pale as bone, its eyes were blank, and in place of a mouth it had only a ragged, broken snout. He had one glimpse before he ran. It towered over her, a man shape with a horse's skull.

3
·
The Knack

Tekker woke late. He saw his clothes in a heap on the floor and sat up suddenly, remembering. He was dressed and downstairs in seconds, on his way out, but his mother stood in the kitchen, barring his way to the door.

'Have you washed?' she said.

'Yes,' he lied.

'Don't you want any breakfast? Have you combed your hair?'

'No and no. Satisfied?'

'Then comb it.'

'It never looks any different.'

'Not to you.' She stood in front of him. 'But it does to me.' She had a smile on her face that he recognized and he knew what was coming. 'And what will *she* think if you're scruffy? Whoever she may be, that is.'

'Oh not again,' he said. She was always teasing him about girls. 'Just because you're all dressed up doesn't mean that I've got to be the same.' Her face was made up and she wore a summer dress, pinched in at the waist with a thin belt. 'Where are you going?'

'Wisbech. It's Saturday.'

He had forgotten. She always went shopping with his father on Saturday, and they stayed there for lunch in a pub on the market-place.

'I've left something for you,' she said. 'It's on the table. Milk's in the fridge.'

'I could have worked that out for myself.'

'Clever little Terence.' She knew he hated being called his full name, but she was as mischievous as any of the girls on the bridge. She handed him the comb. 'Don't forget. We shan't be late; not very.' In a swirl of scented air she was gone.

He let out his breath. Time and everything else seemed confused. It was the middle of the summer holidays, but he should have remembered it was Saturday. He combed his hair; he was right, it didn't make any difference. As soon as he heard the car drive away from the front of the house, he locked up and got his bike from the shed at the bottom of the garden.

There was nobody on the bridge. Too much Saturday traffic. The grass strip between the bowling-club hedge and the football field was deserted, and there was nobody in the little hidden garden around the war memorial. Nobody to talk to about last night. He had slept too late. It would have to be Dan, the disbeliever.

He rode slowly, letting his bike swerve in and out of the grass verge on the road out of the village. He had missed his chance; everybody would have heard Wilf's story by now, and his own version would be diminished. He would never convince anybody.

The Huntleys' house stood well back from the road. It was big and square with a scatter of trees on the lawn in front of it, and a wide gravel drive running by the side to the barn and tractor sheds behind it. The back door was open and Dan's mother heard him on the gravel.

'He's gone swimming,' she called. 'I thought you were with him.'

Tekker shut his eys. Another thing had gone wrong.

He'd forgotten his promise to go swimming. Now it was too late.

Mrs Huntley watched him turn his bike around. 'Tell him his lunch is almost ready.' He raised a hand to show he had heard and rode away. 'Moody young devil,' she said to his back.

Nothing was right. He kicked at his pedals as he rode out along the straight yellow road. He should never have let Wilf Piggins into the secret. He would weaken it. The horse's head would be a horse, nothing else. Damn Piggins. There was more in the world than that idiot believed.

A stone jumped out from under his wheel and skittered along the road. Tekker chased it with his mind, willing it to skip left, then right, and into the verge. It did so. See, Piggins, you thick-head, what you can do if you try.

He felt a small surge of excitement. Perhaps you could nudge things with your mind. Some people believed it. But he had no time for another experiment because already the road was sloping gently up to the green bank that cut across the flat land from horizon to horizon. Beyond it was another bank and between them lay the Middle Level where they swam. There was a narrow bridge that served the farms further out in the fens, and then nothing for miles. A girl's bicycle was leaning against the iron railing and, as he trod on his pedals to reach the top of the slope, Kit climbed up from the bank to stand beside it.

They were surprised to see each other. He and Dan had not invited her swimming.

'I'm trying to get him to come out,' she said. 'It's lunch time.'

He rested his bike beside hers and looked over the railing. Dan's pale limbs straggled in the still water as he floated on his back with his eyes shut.

'Doesn't he look peaceful?' she said.

She had not asked about what happened in the night. Tekker looked away from her into the distance where the endless stretch of water, like a hidden roadway between its banks, vanished into the heat shimmer. She was still punishing him for telling Betty.

'I hardly like to disturb him,' she said. She was still looking down at her brother.

'He looks drowned.' He wanted to hurt her. 'I saw a drowned man once in Wisbech. They pulled him out of the river. He was pale, just like Dan.'

'Dan!' she called. 'It's time to go.'

'He'd been in the water three weeks. There were bits missing. Dan doesn't look alive to me.'

She had her head tilted as she turned towards him and she looked at him from under her eyebrows. Her eyes were dark and accusing. 'You're only doing this because I've said nothing about last night. You want to talk about it more than anything else, don't you?'

'So you are a mind-reader after all.' He was sarcastic.

'It's as plain as anything.'

They were gazing at each other, enemies, when there was a splash from below and Dan's voice.

'What's he doing, Kit? Telling you about the ghost?' Neither of them looked towards him. 'Some ghost! A stray horse. That's all fat Piggins saw.'

So the story had been told. Useless to argue against it now. Tekker let his eyes hold Kit's a moment longer before he looked away. 'Didn't look like a horse to me,' he muttered.

She saw his shoulders droop and suddenly, in spite of herself, felt sorry for him. 'Nor me,' she said.

'What do you know about it? You didn't see it.' And then he remembered that they had both seen it once before, when it was still a secret. 'Anyway you didn't see it last night.'

'I did.' She waited until he faced her. 'I went out to meet you.' Still he did not seem to understand and she felt herself blushing. 'Last night. I was in my Dad's orchard.'

'You saw it?' he asked. 'You were there?' She nodded. 'Does he know?' He pointed at Dan. She shook her head. 'Does Wilf?' Again she shook her head. The hard pupils of his blue eyes were fixed on her. 'And what was it? A horse?'

She drew in her breath, not wanting to answer but there was no escape. 'I don't think so,' she said.

Suddenly he was laughing. 'Of course it wasn't a horse! Only that fool Wilf thinks so. It was something different and we both saw it. You and me.' He was laughing again.

'I don't see what you've got to be so happy about. It frightens me.'

'But Kit, if it really is a ghost, there must be lots of other things that are true.'

'What do you mean?'

'Like mind-reading. We really did that. You and me.'

'Only because we imagined it.' She wanted to stop him.

'And that's not all.' He spun away from her, sweeping his arm wide. 'Look at all that land out there. It looks flat and dull but it's full of things you'd never guess. I feel I could split it wide open like a skin and find something else inside it. It's there, Kit. I know it is.'

'And all because of a horse in a ditch.'

'You want to haul me down.' He was grinning at her. 'Just like your brother. He believes in nothing unless he can touch it. Isn't that so?'

She looked over the railing to see that Dan had swum in his own good time to the far bank and was climbing to where his clothes lay behind some bushes.

'Good old Dan,' Tekker said to his back. 'Nothing much troubles him. Ever.'

Suddenly she did not want to be like Dan. Believing nothing.

'Tekker Begdale,' she said, and he looked towards her. 'I think you're mad.' But she did not raise the tone of her voice and her elbow remained on the railing almost touching his. 'Madder than anybody else I know.'

He understood what she meant, and dipped his head away, gazing down into the water. She was with him. He watched the ripples and said, 'I think just about anything's possible, Kit. You've only got to learn the knack.' He thought of the stone under his bicycle wheel. He knew he had directed its jump. 'I'll prove it,' he said aloud.

'Prove what?'

He pointed to the water below. It was smooth now that Dan had left it, dead flat.

'Watch.' He fixed his eye on their reflection and let his mind push. He felt the coolness of the water's surface, and pushed again. Suddenly, as though a pebble had dropped, the water broke.

'I can do it, Kit!' He pointed at the spreading ripples. 'See that. I'll make it bigger.'

He let his mind reach and push, and suddenly a fresh ripple cut across the rest, arrowed outwards from the shadow of the bridge and sped to the bank where it burst in a flash of sunlight. They were blinded for a moment and then, when they looked up, the whole landscape out beyond the bridge was red in their eyes. As red as a desert. And the sky was purple.

They had turned to face each other, still dazzled, and Tekker was grinning when, from the road sloping down from the bridge, there came the sound of hurrying footsteps and a voice shouting.

4
·
Flare in the Fens

'Was that you?'

The shout came from the foot of the slope. A man was coming towards them, moving as fast as he could but having to lean heavily on a stick and sometimes dragging one foot.

'Did you do that?'

The shout had startled her, but now Kit let out her breath. She knew him. It was Mr Welbeck from the solitary cottage that stood back behind a high hedge of elderberry just where the road began to rise towards the bridge.

'What's old John Welbeck want?' Tekker muttered. 'I'm getting out of here.' But the man saw the movement and gestured.

'Wait!' John Welbeck's narrow face bobbed over his stick as he hurried. 'I've got to have a word with you.'

They watched him. He was a thin man, and his grey hair was cropped close above a face that was pinched in at the temples and cheeks. He would have been tall except for the arthritis that bent him at the hip. Something had made him leave his house without a jacket but, even so, he was neat. His white shirt was buttoned to the wrist and he wore a tie. He stopped in front of them.

'Which of you did it?'

Kit watched his mouth. When he finished speaking, it

shut tight, lipless. He still struggled for breath but fought not to show it.

'Did what?' she asked.

Before he could answer, a sound from the other end of the bridge made them turn. Dan had dressed and was sauntering towards them swinging the water out of his swimming trunks. 'A strange thing just happened,' he said. 'Either my eyes have gone funny or the sky turned red.'

'Yes!' The word snapped from the lipless mouth. 'Which of you did it?'

'Hullo, Mr Welbeck.' Dan could be infuriating. He smiled blandly as though he had just noticed the old man. 'Some trick of the light, I expect. But odd, very odd.'

Kit broke in quickly. 'I saw it as well, but I thought I had just been dazzled.'

There was a pause and the old man's sharp eyes touched each of them in turn like a knife edge.

'So?' he said, and waited a moment. 'Which one of you did it?'

Tekker heard the beginning of a scornful snort in Dan's nose, and said, 'It was just a ripple in the water. I made it flash.'

'Made it?'

'Well . . .' It was more than he had meant to tell. 'We were looking at the water and it dazzled us, that's all.'

'But not me,' said Dan. 'I was behind the bushes. I think it was summer lightning; that sort of phenomenon.'

He went on theorizing, but the old man paid him no heed. From under grey eyebrows his eyes were steady on Tekker. For a few seconds Tekker tried to look away but then gave up the struggle and gazed back at him steadily.

'You. Young man.' The voice snapped at him, ignoring Dan. 'Do you realize what you can do?' Tekker felt the skin of his whole body tingle as though it had suddenly turned silvery thin, but he shrugged. 'Do you not see, you young fool?'

Kit saw John Welbeck's knuckles whiten and she suddenly feared he would strike out, but instead he flicked at the roadway with his stick and scattered pebbles towards the railings. He snatched at Tekker's arm and tugged him towards the edge of the bridge. The scatter of little stones dimpled the water.

'Do it!' he ordered, pointing down. 'Do it again!'

But Tekker pushed back. 'No,' he said. His eyes locked with the old man's, and for a long moment held steady. Then, speaking softly, he said, 'I can't do it to order.'

Dan was exasperated. 'What's all this about?' he said. There was a smile on his face but no amusement. He looked coldly through his spectacles at Tekker and the old man before speaking to his sister. 'They don't seem to want to answer, Kit. Touch of the sun, do you think?'

To hell with you, thought Tekker. And to hell with old John Welbeck. I'll do what I like when I like. He turned away from them. The ripples had gone, but just clear of the shadow of the bridge a brown leaf lay on the glassy surface. He glanced at it, and away. The air was still full of tension. The old man and Dan were glaring at each other, and Kit was on tiptoes, scared of what would happen next.

Tekker scuffed one foot on the ground and it drew their attention towards him. 'I don't know what we're arguing about,' he said, and he kept his voice dull. 'It seems like a lot of rubbish to me.' He went on speaking, using almost meaningless words, not even listening to them himself, but making them keep their eyes on him. And he was looking at Kit. She had a very small nose, and her nostrils were perfect little arches. He concentrated on them and at the same time let his mind loop from the corner of his eye down to the leaf on the water. It was a little brown boat with its ends curled upwards, balanced and ready. His mind reached, and he pushed.

Nothing. He fought to stop himself turning towards it with the full force of his will. Not that; it would not work. The power did not come from the front of his mind. His eyes held Kit's face. The line of her top lip made two tiny hills beneath her nostrils. He let his mind slip sideways, down towards the water. And suddenly it was gone, out of his charge, and the little boat was caught by it. It spun and then slewed across the surface leaving a thin quiver of silver in its wake.

Kit saw his grin. It pointed the corner of his mouth like a devil's. Then a swirl of hot air made her screw her eyes shut.

'Good grief!' Dan spun as the heat caught him, trying to see where it came from, but a red glare dazzled him.

Kit, with her hands over her face, peered between her fingers. Against the deep purple sky, the old man and Tekker stood quite still, gazing directly at each other with their faces lit by the scorching light. She saw Tekker raise his eyebrows, asking a question silently, and John Welbeck nodded curtly. They had agreed on something, and together they turned to look out over the flat land.

'Lightning!' Dan was excited. His glasses were glinting pink. 'It's summer lightning. It's set something on fire.' He shielded his eyes with both hands and searched for the blazing wheat he knew was out there. But it was more than a field. The whole landscape was red; burnt flat. Kit could see no trees or houses. Just a desert of redness. She twisted towards the others. John Welbeck's eyes were piercing the distance as though he was searching for something, and Tekker was drinking it in, unaware of anybody else.

'What's happened?' She knew her voice was tiny and that nobody heard. She looked at her feet. The roadway

was bathed in pink but the gritty surface was still there.
She inched her gaze along it out towards the slope going
down to the fens. She would drive the redness out of her
eyes and see the orchards again. She could already hear
the leaves of the trees. There was a wind gusting sharply
through them, making them rasp. In a moment everything would be normal.

She was already letting out her breath in a sigh when
her eyes saw what was making the sound, and she
screamed.

It was a thin little sound in the back of her throat; a
whimper in a nightmare. The monster in Ma Grist's
garden was out there and coming nearer.

The Horsehead was already beginning its climb up the
slope to the bridge. Its limbs and body were purple-black,
but the long skull, nodding in the pink light, was pale. It
stepped from the furnace below with an insect jerkiness,
and its feet made the noise she heard. Between clawed
toes, bristles scratched the ground.

The old man was closest to her. She flung out a hand as
she screamed and clutched at him. His knuckles closed on
her wrist and held firm. At the same instant he also saw
what was advancing on them.

'No!' His harsh voice rang out, and at the same time he
swung his stick. It struck Tekker across the chest and
made him jerk and spin towards them. His eyes were out
of focus but the old man shouted again to bring him out of
his trance and at the same time shepherded him with his
stick across the bridge and away from the pacing
Horsehead.

They ran, the old man shambling between them, still
clinging to Kit's wrist. She looked back once to see Dan
following, and then the bridge was behind them and they
were stumbling along the road between green fields.

She dragged at the old man until his grip loosened and

E.O.W.—B

she ran ahead, glancing over her shoulder, willing him to catch up, but he slowed and stopped. Tekker was alongside him, and he stood with both hands resting on the handle of his stick with his head bowed as he struggled for breath.

She looked back, panic still leaping in her heart, but the only sound came from Dan's footsteps in the road as he ambled down towards them. The scratching had ceased and the red glow had left the sky.

'Has it gone?' she cried.

'You can see it has.' He glanced casually over his shoulder. 'Sky's blue again.'

'I mean that thing! Didn't you see it?'

Dan, to madden her, swung water from his trunks before he answered. 'What thing do you mean?'

'It was climbing the slope.' She did not dare give it a name.

'Nothing came up the slope that I saw. Too much dazzle.' She was turning to Tekker when Dan spoke again. 'I've changed my mind about summer lightning, by the way. There aren't any clouds to cause it. It's something else. I bet it's something to do with all those planes that have been going over. It was definitely something in the sky. A huge flare, or something. I'm sure I saw a plane.'

'An aeroplane?' The old man's head had jerked up. 'Where? On the ground?'

'No.' There was a faint smile on Dan's face and he pushed his glasses further up his nose. 'In the air. A jet.'

John Welbeck grunted and instantly lost interest. He turned to Tekker, who was standing meekly in the road. 'You,' he snapped. 'You come with me.' He hobbled away a few paces and then barked over his shoulder. 'And bring the others. The girl, at least. She seems to have some sense.'

'A vote of confidence,' said Dan. 'Thanks very much.' But his sarcasm was wasted on the stiff old shoulders that led them across the grass verge and through the gateway in the elderberry hedge to the cottage where John Welbeck lived alone.

The garden was like the man, neat. Vegetables grew on one side of the path and flowers on the other, and the little house rode on a trim raft of lawns edged with tall trees. He paused with one hand on the front door and gave them a frosty smile. 'My fortress,' he said, 'and bolt hole. I think we're safe.'

The sharp grey eyes rested on Kit for a moment and she felt he was encouraging her to smile. She tried, and when he saw it he snorted and pushed the door open, ushering them in ahead of himself.

'First door on the right,' he said. 'Parlour. Make yourselves at home.' As they went through he went past them in the narrow corridor muttering, 'If you want coffee you'll have to wait a moment. Sit down.'

'Damned if I will,' said Dan, just out of earshot of the retreating figure. 'Not in those chairs.'

Kit sat on one of the high-backed chairs against the wall and discovered what he meant. The horsehair stuffing prickled the backs of her legs. But she held herself still and looked around her. The room was small and crowded with heavy old furniture. There was a lot of black; black picture frames and chair seats, a black marble mantel over the fireplace with a black clock; but the woodwork was deep rose-red and shining. It could have been cosy except for the object the boys were looking at.

What they saw was the wooden propeller of an old aeroplane. It hung on the wall opposite the window, close to the ceiling, and the polished amber blades stretched the width of the room.

There was a rattle of cups from the doorway and John Welbeck came in carrying a tray.

'Ha!' He gave a short laugh when he saw where they were looking.

'Why have you got this?' asked Dan.

'Why?' The grey eyebrows came together. 'Because I was a pilot. That's why.'

5
·
The Old Pilot

'I never knew.' Dan's face, under hair still spiky from the river, was surprised. 'When did you fly?'

'First World War. The Great War. No secret about it. No hero stuff, either. I was scared out of my wits.' His head came up like a bird's. 'Ah. The kettle.' They could hear it whistling somewhere at the back of the house and the old man hobbled swiftly out to get it.

Dan turned to Tekker. 'He's not telling us the truth, is he? He's mad.'

Tekker was still pale. He shook his head. 'I don't know about mad,' he said. 'But he was a pilot. I've heard my Dad say.'

'Then how come I know nothing about it?'

Kit's whisper was fierce. 'Because you never listen, that's why! You only hear what you want to hear.' Footsteps were returning. 'Sit down and behave yourself. Don't let that bathing-suit drip all over the floor.'

'Hark at my little sister,' he said, but for once he was obedient, and waited while the old man, with great politeness, measured out coffee for each of them, then milk and sugar. His movements were swift and precise, but Dan's patience broke down.

'When they said you were in the First World War I thought they meant the trenches,' he said.

'And you were right.' He sat himself stiffly at the table

and said one word to each in turn: 'Trenches. Flying. Desert.' His eyes stayed with Tekker on desert, but suddenly he leant back and with his customary abruptness changed the subject.

'Skins,' he said. 'Surfaces. It's all we ever see, most of us.' He smoothed his hand over the glassy polish of the table top. 'My trade,' he said. 'French polisher. Spent most of my life putting a shine on things and that's a kind of deception. It can fool you. Look at the top of this table and you don't see a table. There's the window, see?' He pointed at its reflection. 'And the ceiling. And then deeper down a kind of darkness, like a pool. Deep. Dark. Anything could be there.'

Kit wanted him to stop. She could see the darkness, but the pit was in the old man's mind, dragging her in. Then, alongside her, Dan stirred and John Welbeck's sharp eyes instantly darted at him.

The sudden switch amused Dan, and he laughed, but the old man had finished with him.

'Flying,' he said, and his eyes locked so suddenly on Kit that she felt herself jolt. 'I flew. I had a young lady by then. A very pretty girl. Rather like you. She lived around here.' He made a gesture with his thin fingers, indicating somewhere not far away. 'Somehow the sky seemed the right place to be. Suited my mood, at least. Used to feel closer to her when I flew.' His eyes switched back to Dan. 'Ha! That's a bit fanciful for you, is it? I agree. I was shot down eight times. Shot or crashed, it made no odds, every time put me back in the mud.'

'What were you flying?' Dan asked.

'Old crates mostly. Never any choice. Battered old gridirons.'

'Bristol Scouts,' said Tekker, and when the grey head turned towards him, surprised, he added, 'I saw the picture on your desk. I recognized them.'

Dan glanced at the bureau against the wall. There was a sepia photograph in a silver frame. It showed a group of men in uniform, but there were old biplanes in the background. Only Tekker could have told what they were. 'He's mad on planes,' said Dan. 'He's mad anyway.' And that's why we are here, he thought.

'The Bristol Scout was different,' said John Welbeck. 'I was flying a Scout when it happened.'

'When what happened?' said Dan, but John Welbeck ignored him.

'Nice little aeroplane. Never enough armament, but handled like a dream. I was sent home from France to pick up a new one, and I thought I'd let my young lady see me. Just thought I'd fly over and show off. Do you believe in spells? Do you believe in witches?'

Again the sudden leap, but this time the questions were shot at Tekker. He stayed silent, and Kit took her eyes from the old man to glance at him. Tekker was always claiming marvels, and now the old man was testing him out. But Tekker's mouth remained shut, pulled down at the corners.

'No matter. I don't care what you believe. It's what happens that counts.' Again the nostrils were pinched in as he drew breath. 'And what happened that day changed everything. I was the same as everybody else until then.' His laugh was brief and acid. 'And now I'm the same again. But that day, once and once only, it happened.'

Dan leant forward, about to speak, but John Welbeck merely raised a finger and he was silent.

'Desert,' he said, and the word was meant for Tekker. 'There was no sign of a desert when I flew over to show off. This land is all water, did you know that? It's got silver veins when you fly over it. All those dykes and cuts and canals catch the sun and make a mesh that dazzles you. Dazzles, hah! What dazzled me were sparks in the engine. Sparks, then flames. Both wings on fire, and I was done for. No parachute in those days, stick gone all sloppy and the whole damned fireball out of control. All they'd find would be a little black crisp to bury.'

It amused him, dying. A big laugh at the end. Then his face frosted over again.

'I got lazy, just sitting there waiting for it. I let go of the stick, took my feet off the rudder bar and just looked out along the wings, watching the flames. My word how that canvas burned! Better than kindling. Lovely bonfire.

'The flaps started to trail smoke. Smoke and sparks, and I couldn't budge them to control the damned aeroplane. Got angry then, I remember, and swore at them a bit – *ordered* them to move; told them to pull the nose up a bit.'

His face went as hard as a fist. 'It worked. I told them to move, and they moved. I sat in that cockpit, touching not a thing, not a solitary thing, and hauled that aeroplane's nose up, and flattened her out and brought her down. Then I stepped out without a scratch and watched her burn.'

He allowed the silence to grow for a moment, and then he asked, 'Do you know where I was?'

Dan answered. 'Out there, I suppose. In the fens.'

'Bright red sand? No houses, no trees? Sky deep purple? Was that the fens?'

'You said you were dazzled. The flames must have affected your eyes.'

'Perhaps.' The old man was not interested in Dan's theory. His hand patted the table top as he waited for something from somebody else. Tekker heard his own voice providing it.

'It's still there,' he said. Nobody looked at him; not even John Welbeck. 'The desert is out there. If you can find your way in.'

'I found it once.' Slowly John Welbeck raised his head, as if a jerky movement would break something very fragile. 'I lifted the latch. Just once. Then it shut on me. And I could never get back. Never.'

The room was dim and cool and smelt of polish. Kit had become as still as the chair she sat on.

'All I did was make a leaf move,' said Tekker. 'I knew I could. So I did.'

John Welbeck nodded. 'That's all it takes,' he said. 'A kind of knack. Then it all opens up.'

Dan sighed, and Kit shifted nervously. At any moment her brother would anger John Welbeck and the consequences would be terrible.

'I saw it, too,' she said quickly. 'We all did. You can't deny that.'

'So?' Dan raised his chin. He was haughty. He had already explained everything. Except the ghost – if that's what it was. She had to find out about it.

'Mr Welbeck.' She turned quickly to the old man. 'There was something else.' She held his eyes and the pause dragged on so long that in the end she said faintly, 'There *was* something else, wasn't there?'

It was then that the old man nodded, and it seemed to release Tekker from a daze. His head came up and he said, 'I saw it as well. It had a head like a horse's skull.'

'Oh no, not that!' Dan closed his eyes and scratched his brow. 'Ghosts! I give up.'

But Kit and Tekker were looking at John Welbeck. He had spread his arms and was sitting at the table, his head bowed like a general studying maps. He came to a decision and his head snapped up. 'Pointless to go on with this,' he said. 'We've all been seeing things. An old man dreaming. Stupid of him to pass on all the rubbish in his mind. Dangerous to go any further.'

He stood up, dismissing them, but from the corner of

her eye Kit saw a change come over Tekker. Bright points of colour were in his cheeks, and he leant forward to speak.

'But the desert is there, Mr Welbeck,' he said. 'And I can go back. I can do it any time I want.' He stated it as a slightly surprising fact, as though he had just discovered a talent he'd always imagined but never believed in. 'I'm like you in that aeroplane. I've got the knack.'

Dan snorted. 'Just listen to the lunatic! He believes it all. He thinks that just because something dazzled him out of his wits for a minute he's found another world.' Dan began to enjoy himself, criticizing the old man through Tekker. 'He thinks that anything you're scared into believing is true – even if you bang your head in a crash and see things that aren't there. That's the big mistake, isn't that so, Mr Welbeck?'

It was a risk but he got away with it. The old man stayed silent, leaving Tekker to reply. Kit saw the freckles around his mouth vanish as his face creased and he challenged her brother. 'But what if we *can* go back, Dan?'

'It takes more than a bit of dazzle to fool me.'

Tekker did not argue. The smile vanished but mischief remained. He reached forward, put his cup on the polished table, and sat back looking at it balanced on its own reflection as though it floated in air. It would take very little force to make it slide. 'I've got the knack,' he said. 'We can see what happens.'

'No!' John Welbeck was on his feet. No!'

All three looked up at him, startled.

'You don't know the half of it. There is too much danger.' He stood rigidly, breathing fiercely. But gradually he seemed to become aware of the grimness in his own face and attempted to soften it. He gestured towards Tekker but spoke to Dan. 'If we go on like this, our young friend might start seeing things again, and then where should we be? More coffee?'

He watched them shake their heads and then, speaking seriously to Dan, treating him as the eldest, he said, 'Your theory is a good one. I certainly think so. Visions like that come on swiftly – they have to in a plane crash; no time to think. Then memories add to them and it all builds up. Nothing happens for years, then a bit of sunshine, a flare in the sky and you're off again.'

He was talking in the same vein, agreeing with everything Dan said, but all the time he was easing them out of the house and along the path to the gate.

Tekker tried to catch his eye but failed. Then they were out in the road and the gate was shut between them. It was not until then that John Welbeck's frosty eyes, the tiny pinprick pupils quite steady, rested on him and he said, 'You are lucky to have a friend like this young man.' He nodded towards Dan. 'He's got a good head on his shoulders. Pay heed to him.'

And then he turned and was hobbling back up the path.

6
·
The Fight

Dan was in a good mood as they left the house behind them. 'I'm glad we got that straightened out in the end,' he said. 'Old John Welbeck's not such a fool as he looks.'

'I'll tell him,' said Tekker, 'next time I see him.'

'He put you in your place, young Begdale. Didn't have much to say to you once he and I got onto the truth of it. Just a load of hysteria, that's all.'

'Stop it!' said Kit. 'Don't "young Begdale" him like that. You know it means trouble.'

Dan raised his eyebrows and his thin cheeks creased into a smile. 'Seems little sister has forgiven you, young Begdale,' he said. 'The big crime of telling secrets to Betty Sutton has been forgotten.'

Tekker leant forward to speak to Kit on Dan's other side. 'It's a pity about your poor old brother,' he said. 'He doesn't seem able to grasp things any more. Just rest on my arm, Dan, if you feel tired.'

'Shut up,' she said, 'the pair of you.'

'Ha!' Dan's laugh was a bark. 'When I think what you two have been up to I despair of the younger generation. Men with horses' heads. Red deserts. And all of it hanging about, just waiting to be opened up like the pages of a book. Tekker, my young friend, you are a poet; you have turned my little sister's head.'

Tekker, pushing his bike, walked on a few paces before he looked across at Kit. 'Shall I bring it back?'

She thought for a moment, looking at the ground, and then spoke seriously. 'Not now,' she said. 'I think that when we try it again we've got to be ready for it. In the right place, and everything like that.'

'Good grief!' Dan smote his head and stood stockstill. 'They believe it! They really believe it!' He looked from one to the other. 'And take that idiotic grin off your face, Begdale.'

Tekker knew his face had gone round with pleasure, like a full moon, but he didn't care. Kit was on his side.

'Hell's bells!' Dan refused to let them move on. 'Things have come to a pretty pass.'

'Just listen to the poor old man,' Tekker said kindly. 'He's had a nasty shock.'

Dan ignored him. 'What we really need is independent witnesses. Somebody like . . .' he searched his mind, 'Wilf Piggins. He's the fellow. Convince Wilf and you'd convince anybody.'

'You wouldn't!' Kit cried. 'You haven't got to tell *anybody*!'

'That's wiped the smiles off your faces.' Dan was pleased with himself. 'Yes, I really must approach friend Piggins. Good, sensible Wilf.'

'If you do,' she said fiercely, 'I'll never utter a word to you as long as I live!'

'What a relief. But never mind, you'll always have Tekker to talk to. I can guarantee that, no matter what happens.'

'What do you mean?' She was suspicious.

'Oh didn't you know?' Dan spoke airily. 'Young Begdale told me once he thought you were quite pretty.' She dipped her head, and he went on, 'There's no need to blush – only *quite* pretty, he said, not *absolutely* pretty;

that would be impossible.' He was enjoying the effect he was having on both of them. 'He likes the way your nose doesn't stick out very much. That seems to sum up your qualities as far as he is concerned. A blunt little nose. Still, kingdoms have been lost and won for less.'

'I could zap you,' said Tekker.

'You see, Kit, he doesn't deny it.'

'You're a traitor, Huntley.'

'I always aim to please.'

Suddenly Kit was riding away from them as fast as she could, her head forward and her hair streaming.

'You certainly do your best to spoil things,' said Tekker.

Dan's face wore its superior smile. 'A little truth-telling never hurt anyone.'

'You're too damned cocky,' said Tekker, but nothing ruffled Dan.

'I could tell you what my sister thinks of you.'

'Don't bother.'

'Careful, young Begdale, I just might not say a word.' He watched as Tekker looked away, pretending to be indifferent. 'But I think I shall, as it's not very flattering.' He waited until, very gradually, Tekker turned towards him. 'She thinks you exaggerate.'

Tekker stared back at him, and slowly moved his features until he was giving his imitation of somebody pressing his face against a window pane, flattened.

'You do that very well.' Dan did not smile. 'Mind you, it's a big advantage to start with a face like a boxer dog, somewhat squashed. That's something else she said.'

'I don't exaggerate.'

Dan shrugged.

'I've never told her anything that didn't happen. Never.'

'Well,' said Dan, 'all I can tell you is that she thinks you're wild. But then, everybody thinks that.'

Tekker's back wheel skidded in the sandy road as he trod

hard on the pedals and took off. Kit was already out of sight, but he did not want to catch her. He needed to be alone. Dan watched him dwindle into the distance, and sauntered homeward swinging water from his trunks.

*

There was a lot to think about. Too much. Tekker pushed back the cloth from the lunch his mother had left on the kitchen table, put sauce on the cold sausages, honey on the bread, and ate them all with cheese. The slices of cucumber he regarded as only a decoration, and he left them.

He went upstairs and lay on his bed, looking up at his aeroplanes hanging on threads from the ceiling in a dogfight. They were a mixture from both wars but one of them, an SE5A, was similar to a Bristol Scout. He lay, watched it sway, and flew it, imagining the tilt and swoop along the wall, the dive past the curtains, and a bumpy, puttering landing on the carpet. What if he really tried to make it move? He was about to nudge it with his mind when he suddenly shut his eyes. No more of that. Not yet.

The edge of the cockpit had a rim of stitched leather. It was oiled and supple under his hand as he leant over to look back along the fuselage. The stiff canvas, laced tight to the frame, drummed slightly even though there was no rush of air. He was poised on the lip of a stall, held fast against the harsh, high blue of the sky. He was treading air.

Suddenly flame flickered and he dipped into a dive. The wind screamed in the struts and he was helpless.

'Terry!'

He woke with a start.

'Terry are you there!' It was his mother's voice from the foot of the stairs. And then he heard her say to his father, 'That boy's gone out again without locking the door. Just wait till I catch him.'

Drastic measures were needed. He jumped off the bed.

'Mother!' He was at the top of the stairs, posed dramatically. They looked at each other for a moment and, as he guessed, it worked.

'My son!' Even though she was carrying two shopping bags she made an effort to open her arms.

'Mother! So you've come home!'

He plunged down the stairs and knelt in front of her.

'My curly-headed child!' She made an effort to put a hand on his head but something spilled from one of her shopping bags and she looked towards her husband just inside the door. 'The young bugger's got round me again.'

'You ought to be on the stage, you two.' His father was looking at the remains of Tekker's lunch. 'Don't you like cucumber?'

'Left it for you.'

'Rabbit food,' said his father but picked it off the plate.

Now was the time to question them, when they were bustling about after market-day in Wisbech.

'I didn't know a plane had crashed out beyond the Pingle,' he said.

'When?' His mother was startled. 'This afternoon?'

'First World War,' he said, and she lost interest. He looked at the tattoo on his father's arm. That was the Navy and the last war, but he might know. 'It crashed in flames,' he said.

His father had two bags of flour in his big hands. 'You know where that goes,' said his wife and pointed at the corner cupboard.

He wandered over towards it, thinking, and then said, 'I reckon you're right, Tekker.'

'Terry,' his wife corrected him, but he did not seem to hear.

'I've heard the old boys down at the Bells say something about that. Pilot got killed.'

'No,' said Tekker.

'Well that's what I heard. It was either that or they never found him; one or the other.'

'It was old John Welbeck.'

'It never was,' said his mother.

'Oh yes,' said his father. 'Old John was a pilot all right, but he don't hardly talk about it. Couldn't have been him, though. He's not dead yet.'

'He's certainly not,' she said. 'That old devil's got a glint in his eye still.'

Tekker's father winked at him. 'Your mother would know,' he said.

'Well I do. And so do a lot of other people. He was a fine looking man I should think, once. And he had a girl-friend. Did you know that?' Her husband shook his head. 'And did you know she vanished? No, I know you didn't. And I'll tell you something else for nothing. That's why he lives out there where he do, all alone, to be near where she used to live.'

She paused, stacking things from her shopping bags on the table. 'And I'll tell you one more thing I bet neither of you knows. His young lady had a sister, and that sister was right jealous because she had her eye on John Welbeck herself. And she's still alive, but you'll never guess in a thousand years who it is.'

Even before he heard her say it, Tekker knew.

'Ma Grist,' she said.

*

It was the usual Saturday night crowd by the bridge and Tekker was late, deliberately. He did not want to face Kit after what Dan had told her. She was below the bridge on the bank and when she saw him she looked away quickly.

Dan was on the bridge, only a pace or two away from Wilf Piggins, and Wilf was grinning.

'Ain't seen much of you today,' he said to Tekker. 'Been recovering, have you? I didn't realize you was so badly scared last night.'

'Wasn't me who was scared.' Tekker leant on the railing with Dan between himself and Wilf. 'I hung about after you'd run off.'

'That you never!' Wilf raised his voice to address everybody. 'Once I'd scared that horse out o' the ditch, he vanished. Never saw him again.'

'That wasn't a horse,' said Wilf's hanger-on, Lenny. 'That was a nightmare.' He was pleased with that. 'Tekker Begdale's nightmare!'

Wilf permitted himself a smile, but no more. He pushed himself back from the railing, still holding it with both hands, and hunched his shoulders. 'What interests me a bit more than that,' he said, 'is something else that Begdale can do.'

'What's that, Wilf?'

'I just heard about this.' Wilf took his time. The folds of his face glistened. 'He can move things, can Begdale. He can move them by just looking at 'em.'

Tekker saw Kit's head jerk up, and she scrambled to her feet shouting to Dan on the bridge above. 'What have you said! I told you to say nothing!'

Dan was unperturbed. He turned to Tekker. 'All I did was to ask if he saw the sky turn red today. It would have been interesting to know, as both of you have seen something in the night, even if it was only a horse.' He was quite calm. 'But as it turned out, the sky stayed the same for him all day. Then I had to tell him a bit more, of course.'

'I wish you hadn't,' said Tekker.

'Well so do I, in a way.' It was the nearest Dan had come to an apology. 'But nevertheless it would be interesting to see what would happen if you tried the trick again.'

'Yeah,' said Wilf. 'It would.'

'Not for him.' Anger pinched Tekker's mouth tight. 'Not now. Not ever.'

Skinny Lenny backed up his master. 'Come on, Begdale. Show us your stuff. Make us a ripple.' He pointed down at the still water.

So Dan had told them even that. Tekker frowned, and Lenny's eyes could not hold his. 'I don't do anything,' he said, 'for you, or anybody like you.'

Wilf's temper went. 'If I tell you to do something, Begdale, you do it!' He stooped swiftly, picked up a stone and hurled it into the still water below. 'There's a bloody ripple, Begdale. Now you do it.'

It was an order. Anger dappled Wilf's cheeks pink and white.

'Do it!'

Tekker's breath hissed as he drew it in. 'Not for you, fatty,' he said.

There was a soundless instant like the tiny pause before an explosion. Then Wilf's bulk moved.

He did not fight like anybody else. He came straight forward with his hands in front of him and his fingers spread like claws. And he was fast. Tekker lunged sideways but was too slow. One claw caught his face.

The thumb was in his cheek pulling the corner of his mouth back. The other hand had him by the shirt collar and was pulling the other way. Tekker could feel the inside of his cheek tearing. He reached up and grabbed at both wrists, using all his strength to press them inwards. But the claw tightened, making more damage, and he could not stop a thin cry at the back of his throat.

Wilf heard it and heaved forward. Tears of pain flooded Tekker's eyes. He could hardly see. But just enough. Wilf dipped his head and Tekker, using his grip on both wrists for leverage, lunged. His skull rode into the middle of the fat face. He felt flesh squash against bone, and struck again.

The grip on his cheek loosened and fell away. Suddenly Wilf was having to fend him off. Tekker went after him. There was blood in his mouth. He tasted it as his fist hit solid flesh. Wilf's head came forward, and Tekker's shoulder went down as he put his weight behind the punch. It was scientific. His knuckles jarred against bone, and Wilf sat down.

Tekker stood over him. Suddenly his arms were weak, and Lenny was tearing at him. Dan pulled him from Tekker's back but he struggled and yelled, 'He was hitting him when he was down! I seen him, I seen him!'

Piggins raised himself on one knee and Tekker stood back ready for the rush he would never be able to stop. But blood was running from Wilf's nose to his mouth and then his chin. His eyes did not meet Tekker's. He was beaten.

And suddenly all Tekker's anger flooded away. 'You all right?' he asked.

The doggy brown eyes flicked up, then away and a spark of courage stirred. 'You still can't do it,' he said.

'Of course he can't!' screamed Lenny. 'He's a bloody fake! He's just a rotten, lousy fake!'

Tekker turned his back on them and walked away along the churchyard wall until its curve put them out of sight.

7

·

The Red Desert

'Your face!' Kit caught up with Tekker and stopped him. 'He only just missed your eye!'

The rage of the fight had not left him and he felt no pain until he smiled. He winced. 'At least I got in a few,' he said.

'Yes.' She wanted to say that Wilf deserved it, but the fight had frightened her and she wanted no more. 'But it serves you right. You shouldn't keep saying things nobody can believe.'

'Thanks.' He wiped blood from his face with his wrist. 'That's a real help.'

'I didn't mean it like that.'

'You said nobody believes me. That means you as well.' He saw her mouth open and knew he had hurt her, but could not stop himself. 'You're just the same as everybody else.'

She felt tears begin to sting her eyes but fought them. She was still trying to think of how she could reply when Dan strolled up. He examined Tekker, standing back, and said, 'Your beauty, such as it was, has been badly damaged. The boy Wilf gave you quite a mauling.'

'Oh did he? I didn't think I did too badly.'

'Matter of opinion. He still lives.'

Kit watched Tekker's battered face darken. He had expected praise and was getting indifference. Dan made it worse.

'You'll really have to watch the things you say, young Begdale. Especially to people like Wilf. They haven't your imagination.'

'You're just like your sister.' There was still blood at the corner of Tekker's mouth. His frown had deepened. 'The pair of you. You don't see a damned thing. Not even when it's staring you in the face.'

Dan smiled. 'Not red deserts, anyway.'

'Oh what's the use!' Tekker turned his back and left them. When they began to argue, he broke into a trot.

'See what you've done!' Kit rounded on her brother. 'You didn't give him any credit for standing up to that great big bully – and beating him.'

'Little sister.' Dan was at his most maddening. 'It's not *my* praise he wants; it's yours.'

'Oh shut up!' She began to move away, too angry to stay.

'When you catch him up,' he called, 'you can add my congratulations. I thought he did quite well.'

She had to put things right, but Tekker was moving swiftly, heading out from the village, away from home. When she saw him go past her house without a glance she almost gave up the chase, but then she realized he was making for John Welbeck's lonely cottage. In this mood he would seek out danger wherever he found it, and the old man might help him.

He paused at the gateway and looked back before he opened it but, when he saw her, he changed his mind and climbed the slope to the bridge.

She followed, and caught up with him after he had crossed over. They were the only two people in the whole flat landscape but he continued walking as though he had not seen her.

'Tekker,' she said. 'Dan says he's sorry.'

He grunted, and for a while they kept pace, with the narrow road between them. It was getting dark. She heard a motorbike far away, cruising into the distance, and then fall into silence somewhere near the horizon.

'Dan doesn't bother me,' he said. 'I know he'll never change.'

She let a few paces go by before she replied. 'You mean me, don't you? You think I don't believe you can . . .' She wanted him to finish saying it, but he remained silent. 'You want somebody else to believe your mind can make things happen, don't you?'

'John Welbeck believes it, no matter what he says when Dan is there.'

'I don't care about Mr Welbeck. He's just an old man.'

Tekker stopped so suddenly she went on a pace and had to turn.

'I could prove it, Kit. I could prove it now.'

'No, I don't want you to.' She paused and then spoke reluctantly. 'Mr Welbeck said it's dangerous. It makes other things happen.'

Tekker laughed. 'But John Welbeck doesn't matter. He's just an old man.' He let the sarcasm sink in, and then his sullen mood changed and his battered face was suddenly lively. 'Anyway we've come to no harm so far, and I think he's like us in some ways. I watched him when you were talking to him. He couldn't take his eyes off you, and I know why.'

'I didn't notice anything.'

'I think you must be just like his girl-friend.'

'Now you're being silly.'

'No I'm not. And if you are like her, then you can make things happen – just like me.'

'I can't. I know I can't.'

He did not reply. He let his eyes leave her, and she followed his glance to where a small white flower grew in the verge. It was balanced on a thin stem at the height of her knee and even in the still air seemed on the point of trembling. She knew what he meant her to do.

'Try,' he said. 'All you've got to do is look away from it and let your mind give it a push.'

It was a tiny thing to do, but she was afraid. 'No,' she said, but her eyes remained on him and the possibility began to tempt her. She fought it, concentrating on his face. One side was bruised and lopsided, and the grainy light almost hid his freckles. She absorbed the details but did not really see him for, in spite of herself, her attention was on the floating whiteness of the flower. She knew she could not make it stir. It was out of the question. Impossible. She let her mind creep towards it. I'll prove nothing happens. Nothing at all. Even while the words were in her head she let her mind reach for the flower and tug.

It was instantaneous. As though some creature was pushing at its roots, the flower quivered slightly. She twisted to see what caused it, and as she did so the white bloom whipped sideways.

She jumped back, and her sudden movement seemed to tear a membrane of the fading light. A red glare and a storm of heat swirled around them. They screwed up their eyes to see through the dazzle. Like a gong, the setting sun blazed in the deep blue sky, and under it the land was red. Red sand. It was humped and smooth except where red rocks jutted like ribs of wrecked ships and threw purple shadows. No houses. No trees. Nothing moved. It was a furnace floor burned to red ash.

Then a breeze, almost visible, threw a wisp of sand at Kit's legs and she wrenched herself round to make sure Tekker was there.

'You did it!' The breeze died under his voice in a faint hiss. 'We've done it, Kit! We're right through.'

The silence seeped into them and they turned, almost back to back, searching for clues, for a way out. There was no road. The bridge had vanished. Only far away, on the horizon, there was a faint wrinkle that may have been hills. They were in a desert, tiny and alone.

Kit had hardly moved her feet, as though the place she stood marked the way back. She closed her eyes. When she opened them, the illusion would have vanished.

'Kit! Look!'

He tugged at her arm and she lost her place on the sand. He was pointing. Not far from them, just beyond an outcrop of red rock, something jutted from the desert.

'It's the bridge,' she said. 'It must be.' It seemed to be in the wrong direction, but it was a structure and she could see ribs like railings. Every step would make it more real, and soon the glare would fall away and they would be back in the grey twilight.

'Come on.' He was pulling at her hand. 'I knew it was there.'

The sun pressed with a hot, hard finger between their shoulder blades and pushed their shadows out ahead. Pebbles lay on the sand. Kit concentrated on them. In a moment she would see that they were scattered on the hard road. But each pebble lay at the point of a little vee in the sand where the wind had blown the grains. She kicked at one to drive the sand away, but it skipped ahead of her, leaving a trail of dimples. The desert was real.

They came to the first of the boulders. It was worn smooth and lay like a huge egg in its own pool of shadow. The heat seemed to sing around it, and Tekker felt sweat trickle down the side of his nose. He wiped it off and the pain of his cuts surprised him. The normal world was only a skin's distance away. They had to hurry before it came back.

'Not far now,' he said. It was vital to reach the structure before everything was snatched away. 'We can reach it.'

More boulders lay on the surface like the heads of gigantic seals, an endless school of them swimming their way, each pushing up a bow wave of sand and leaving behind twists of red ripples. Suddenly Kit stopped. She was sure the heads had moved.

'Wait!' She held his arm. The rounded shapes, many as tall as themselves, lay still. She had been tricked by the way they overlapped. 'It was nothing,' she said, but still in the corner of her eye there seemed to be a flicker of movement far away to the right as though something was keeping pace. She twisted again, but everything was motionless.

A gentle slope now, and the structure was closer. They must be climbing to the bridge. Tekker was running and she went with him, away from the boulders, to the top of the sand dune where the structure made a pattern against the sky. Ten paces from it, they stopped. Tekker was excited.

'I knew we'd find it, Kit, it's exactly where it should be.'

If it was a bridge there would have been water beyond the slope. There was sand without end, and the shape bridged nothing. It was a fragile honeycomb of thin struts, all as yellow as old bones, jutting uselessly from the sand.

'I can't make it out.' She hung back. 'It's like a skeleton.'

'Sort of.' He was almost laughing, and she went forward with him, reluctantly. 'Now can you see?'

Quite suddenly it took shape. 'It's an aeroplane!' She could see now that one side was embedded in the sand, and the bare spars of one pair of wings were tilted at the sky. And she knew what aeroplane it was. 'It's John Welbeck's.'

'Burnt out,' he said. 'Nearly all its canvas has gone.' Barely a shred remained. The blowing sand had flayed everything from the wooden struts that had survived the flames and the crash and had polished them. One wheel was buried, and the black tyre of the other was cracked and perished. 'It's beautiful!' he said.

Kit was a pace or two nearer the engine and the

fractured propeller. Her eyes followed the spars along the fuselage from the tail to the cockpit until she saw the metal back of the pilot's seat. And something else.

Tekker saw her stiffen. She blocked his view, and he moved to one side. Then he saw it. Lolling sideways, one arm over the cockpit edge, there was a body.

The desert was more silent than a closed room. Even their breath seemed to stir no air. The only movement was the heave of their hearts, deep inside. They had got everything wrong. There should be no pilot in John Welbeck's Bristol Scout.

Tekker stepped nearer, put out a hand and touched the fuselage next to the tail. It was hot, as though the fire that had made it crash had at that moment burned itself out, and it trembled. He shook it, but the hunched shape in the cockpit remained slumped where it had come to rest. It had happened long ago. The pilot would be no more than a skeleton. Yet the shape was solid.

He moved slowly along the wreck. The arm that hung over the edge had no hand. And there was no head. It was the drowned man all over again.

Kit saw him hesitate and went up to him. There was no need to go any closer. There were more urgent dangers. She was about to draw him back when something about the body seemed even more strange. Almost instantly she knew what it was and, giving herself no time to think, she went past Tekker and reached up at the dangling arm. She tugged, and the whole shape pivoted on the edge of the cockpit and fell. She jumped back as it hit the sand at her feet, but at the same time, as though to convince herself, she said, 'It's a coat, that's all. Just a coat.'

It was leather, stiffened with age. Its long skirts lay straight, but one arm was bent upwards.

'A flying coat!' Tekker bent over it. 'Of course it is.' He was examining the worn patches and the places where oil had soaked into it, but there were no scorch marks. John

Welbeck must have thrown it back into the cockpit after the crash. 'His gloves are still in the pocket!' He stooped and eased them out. The long gauntlets must have reached half way to the pilot's elbow. The fingers, protected by the pocket over many years, were still supple. He put the gloves on the sand and knelt beside the coat. 'I wonder if there's anything else.'

It was like finding an ancient tomb and searching it for treasure. He put his hand into the pocket and felt the cloth lining. It was very fragile, and he felt it tear as he eased his fingers deeper.

'What's this?'

Kit saw him sit back and hold something up. For one ugly moment it seemed that a grotesque head dangled from his fingers – two huge eyes and a gape beneath. She gasped and clenched her fists, but then the sun glinted in the dead eyes and she saw they were two discs of glass.

'A flying helmet,' he said. 'An old leather one, and it's still got the goggles round it.'

He handed it to her and she forced herself to take it. The crumpled leather was soft, and so were the padded rims of the goggles. He stooped again, oblivious to everything except the coat, but she had seen enough. They had to get away from this dreadful place. She turned to look back.

The boulders were like sphinx heads now, their noses and lips worn away by centuries of sand, but still watching. There was an army of them, stretched in a band across the desert, half submerged and all motionless.

Then, far away to the left, her eyes tricked her again. One of the boulders seemed to stir. She jerked her head towards it to make certain. It was quite still. But there was movement. It came from something else.

On thin legs, the spidery man shape paced between the rocks, its long skull nodding as it came.

8
·
The Flying Helmet

Their only shelter was the boulders. They ran until the shadow of the first fell on them and then they crouched. Panting, they looked at each other. Panic began to leap, but they fought it.

'We got in, Kit,' he said. 'We can get out the same way.'

She bit her lip and nodded. It had to be now. It had to work.

There were no ripples, no trembling flowers to push with his mind and turn the key to let them out. He picked up a handful of sand and threw it. As the grains hissed down he kept his eyes on hers, but at the same time he made his mind reach outwards, pushing at the rain of falling sand. When he split its curtain they would walk through into the cool evening, safe in the roadway.

He was already standing up, confident of moving out, when the last of the sand reached the ground. But there was nowhere to go. The desert remained. They tried together, but they were listening for footsteps, and their concentration was gone. Nothing happened.

'It won't work!' He was muttering to himself. 'I can't do it!'

She watched him try once more, but knew it would fail. She had a tiny core of ice and was thinking.

'We're in the wrong place,' she said. 'We've got to find the spot where we stepped through.' He began to break away, but she held him, watching the Horsehead. It was closer, but finding no straight route through the boulders. She waited until it dipped for a moment out of sight, and then she called, 'Run!'

They flung themselves to the shelter of the next shadow.

'We've got to find our trail.' She gasped for breath. 'Then we'll know where we are.'

Tekker nodded. It could not be far. He eased himself up the face of the boulder to see if the way was clear. He saw the bobbing crest of bristles and slid back, but too late. The empty sockets were turned full on him.

He snatched at her, and together they broke from cover. They ran from boulder to boulder, the sand clogging their feet and making them stumble. Then he heard her choke a word and point. Away to one side, where the boulders ended, were the marks of the way they had come.

They veered together and ran towards the trail, but now they could hear the swish of footsteps behind them. Their old footmarks were clear, but the sand was softer and their feet sank deeper. They laboured, the hot air burned their throats, and they blinked away sweat.

The footprints ended. This was the place. The doorway was here. They looked back. The Horsehead had cleared the boulders and was pacing the red sand.

'I can't do it by myself.' His words were gabbled. 'You've got to help.'

He stooped to pick up a handful of sand and flung it. It fanned out against the blue sky and they bowed their heads until their foreheads touched and willed it to blow wider. But they knew it was useless. Their thoughts stayed with them. The sand fell back.

The Horsehead was angling across the sand between them and the shelter of the rocks. They saw it lift its ragged snout as though it sniffed them, and they ran, driven before it, further into the open.

A dune rose beneath them and they staggered. Their feet thrust but the sand slid backwards and they were on the treadmill, running but slowed to walking pace. The sun rested on the dune's top and blinded them. They scrambled towards it. At the top they could run again.

They were almost there when their last hope went. Over the edge of the dune a shape rose to meet them.

They stopped, half crouched on the slope. Now they were prey. Defenceless.

They began to slither sideways. It was a last, useless twitch. But even that was stopped. The figure above them raised both arms. It carried a weapon, and it had a voice.

'Here!' The cry reached them through the hot air. 'Here! This way!'

The figure's arms were wide. The weapon was not aimed at them.

'Run!'

Below them, the dipping head was close. They pushed themselves upright, plunging through the sand. But the ground was hard underfoot and they were running. Darkness spread outwards around them, and cool air. They were on a road, and the grass in the dark verges whipped at their legs. Above them, John Welbeck stood on the bridge, his stick raised like a sword.

Kit flung herself at him, both arms around his waist and pressed her head against his chest. She looked back.

The grey road wandered out into the fens and merged with the darkness. A few stars blinked in the passive sky, and beneath it nothing moved.

She shuddered, and the old man put an arm around her shoulders.

'Young fools,' he said, but there was little harshness in his voice. He lowered his stick. 'It almost got you.

Another second . . . just a few paces . . . Far too damned close.'

'I know.' She realized she was still clasping him round the waist, and released him. She was suddenly shy. 'Sorry,' she said.

He took his arm away from her shoulder as though he had noticed nothing, and his head was turned away, listening to Tekker.

'We did it, though.' Tekker was crouched in the roadway, still panting. 'We got there. And out again.'

'If it hadn't been for me you would have stayed there!' John Welbeck rapped the ground.

'Would we?' Tekker looked up.

'Of course you would!' The old man glared down at him. 'You're an idiot, boy! You are meddling with things that will destroy you – you and this girl here.'

Tekker, still crouching, was picking at the ground with a fingernail, trying to ease a pebble from the tar. It was hard and real, and it would not budge. It was the kind of evidence Dan would accept. And Dan was never in danger. The sickening fear swept over him again and he looked back. Nothing but the fens. The rest was imagination. They saw it because they wanted to, and because the old man encouraged them. He stood up. 'There is no danger,' he said. 'Nothing will ever get us. We'll always get away.'

'I fail to understand you, boy.'

'I reckon Dan's right. We've been fooling ourselves. It's flares, or something. We get blinded and imagine the rest of it. We never get touched.' He put a hand to his swollen cheek. 'Except me.' He tried to grin, but nobody was amused.

John Welbeck grunted. 'You switch about too quickly for me, young man. First one way, then another.'

'What Dan said makes sense.'

'I see. That means you are blaming me.' John Welbeck

drew in his breath. 'My ancient brain. If I didn't encourage you to see all this, you wouldn't see it. Is that it? And I'm too old to know what I'm doing. Is that what you're trying to tell me? Too old? Too damned old?'

Tekker did not reply, and Kit saw him and the old man face each other, staring coldly. Their anger was mixed with a kind of fierce sadness, as though each was draining the spirit out of the other and knew it.

'Don't!' She took a step forward. 'Don't do this. You're saying things you don't mean, both of you.' Her own boldness surprised her. 'I don't care whether it's real out there, or not. It doesn't matter.'

She had raised a hand as though to put a barrier between them, and as she did so she became aware she was grasping something. She had a strap between her fingers. And something was swinging from it. Twisting slowly, so that its blank eyepieces caught the dim light, was the flying helmet.

She let John Welbeck unlace the strap from her fingers and take it. His gaze swept the flat landscape just once, then he turned his back on it and led them down from the bridge to his cottage.

Tekker allowed himself to be led. There had been no flying helmet in the road. It was impossible. In a daze, he walked beside Kit, following the old man as he took them around the back of the house. A light showed through the small panes of one window and the back door stood ajar, spilling more light onto the path.

'I came out in a hurry,' said the old man and pushed the door wider to let them in.

The light came from a reading-lamp with a glass shade in the corner. A high-backed armchair stood alongside it, and a fire glowed under a tall mantelpiece.

'Sit down.' John Welbeck removed a newspaper from a footstool, and swung a black kettle on a little iron platform over the fire, where it sang gently through everything that followed but he never got round to making them a drink.

'My guard room,' he said. 'Everything to hand.' He had made the small room cosy. There was one other armchair, a table, bookshelves in alcoves, and an open door in the corner through which Kit saw the shelves of a larder. John Welbeck stirred the coals. 'An old man gets cold if it's a long watch.'

At last, Tekker's eyes focused and he glanced swiftly at the window. John Welbeck noticed.

'I can see the river bank from here,' he said. 'It's necessary. Things are happening.' Once again he motioned them to sit down, and he eased himself into the chair by the reading-lamp. It was not until then that he paid any attention to the flying helmet. He turned it over a few times in his hands, then put it on the arm of his chair and waited to be questioned.

'It's yours, isn't it?' Tekker, sitting on the footstool, had pushed himself as far back as he could to be away from the old man.

'Of course.' John Welbeck's back was very straight, but his hand had an old man's tremor. 'If it wasn't for this,' he patted the helmet, 'I would have sent you home – if I thought you would have gone.' The thin smile came and went. 'But now you know too much. You have seen my Bristol Scout. You know I speak the truth.'

'All right.' Tekker stood up. He had to be ready for whatever was coming. 'What's been happening to us?'

Kit watched the old man in his chair and saw him wave his hand for Tekker to sit down again, but she hardly believed it was happening. She saw Tekker perch himself on the table, one leg swinging, and she made herself speak.

'What is it?' Her voice was little more than a whisper, and she swallowed hard and spoke louder. 'Witchcraft?'

The ridiculous word brought the keen eyes to her. 'Of a

sort,' he said. 'Dangerous.' His pauses were as brief as his
sentences. 'I doubted it until you found it all again.
Found it, just as we did.'

'Who?' she asked.

'She was called Stella. She lived far out in the fens – she
and her family in a little house. More like a brick hut than
a proper house; had an earth floor, I remember. But
remarkable people – Stella and her sister and her mother.
Just the three; her father was long since dead. But you
always felt they knew something; something special;
something they weren't saying.'

His mouth shut as though he had finished, but
suddenly he was speaking again.

'Stella and me. We grew fond of each other; more than
fond.' His eyes blazed with a kind of anger at them
because they were so young and he was being forced to tell
them things he told nobody. 'I loved her. She loved me,
and she tried to tell me what she knew.'

Once again the quick pause as if he doubted what to
tell. But his mind was made up, and he faced them both.

'Out in the fens, living alone, those three women
discovered something. They could see what I could not
see. Wonderful things. She tried to show me. We would
walk along a lane and she would suddenly say there were
shining houses on both sides. I saw nothing. Or there was
a glittering mountain that went up to the sky.' He snorted. 'A mountain in the fens! It was never there for me.
Never. She tried to show me how to see it. Just let your
mind push, she said, and a door will open. She tried to
make me do it, but I never could. I could not believe.

'Then came the day we told her mother about ourselves. She said nothing. Not one word. But she went to a
drawer and took out something black and flat and round
and put it in Stella's hand. I thought it was a purse,
money for us to get married. No such thing. It was a piece
of black wood, bog oak dug up from the fen, thousands of

years old and hard as stone. Just a black disc.

'Not a word was said, but something had happened. I could tell it by looking at them. Stella took me outside and turned the disc in my hand. I saw it had a picture scratched on it. It looked like a city, but it wasn't very clear, I couldn't make it out. Then she said, "You can look up now. You can see!"'

John Welbeck sat rigidly straight. 'And I did. I saw it all. Right in front of me. A palace. And a mountain. All blazing in the sun. It was there I tell you, there!' He thumped the arm of his chair. 'We walked into it, seeing marvellous things, again and again. I have never been so happy. Never.'

A quick intake of breath narrowed his nose. 'So why am I not there now? What happened? I shall tell you.' A quick stab of the eyes. 'Her sister found out. Her elder sister. I have never seen such pain in a face. She had thought I loved her. That she was going to show me the palace, not Stella. I saw her pain, and then I felt her fury. I still feel it. She drove me out of that palace and nothing that Stella nor her mother could do was equal to her hatred. It was like a storm that swept us, and the war came and helped her. I was snatched away.'

He stopped speaking, and this time the silence grew. His attention was far away, until Kit stirred in her chair. He looked at her. 'You know the sister,' he said.

Kit nodded. 'Ma Grist.'

'Your name for her, not mine.'

There was another question, and Kit whispered it. 'Stella?' she asked.

The ferocity in the old man jerked him forward in his chair. 'She's still there!' His arm shot out, pointing to the window and the fens outside. 'Trapped in that place.'

Tekker eased himself from the table and stood up. 'How do you know?' he said.

John Welbeck sat back in his chair. 'Because of you,' he

said. 'You have the trick of the mind that I never had, and you found it.'

'Red sand,' said Tekker. 'I didn't see a palace.'

'But it is there, young man. And my Stella is inside it. Trapped there by her sister.' He was speaking calmly now, certain that he was believed. 'Their mother died and her sister grew strong. I was away at the war and I never knew, until that day I crashed. I discovered the trick of the mind as I was near death and found the desert. There had been no desert with Stella. Only wonderful things. But a change had come. There was a desert now. And creatures in it.'

'Horseheads.' Tekker said the word softly, and the old man nodded. The room had become chilly.

'They drove me out. And once I was out I could never find my way back. I tried again and again but nothing happened. I had lost the one thing that could let me in once more. The black disc had helped me. I carried it because Stella gave it to me. But I lost it when I crashed.' His jaw muscles clenched and his face seemed no more than bone. 'I lost it!'

Kit's eyes shifted to the helmet and goggles on the arm of his chair. 'It's still out there, Mr Welbeck,' she said. 'We could find it for you.'

'No!' The command was barked at her. 'I absolutely forbid it. You have wandered into something that is none of your affair!' He held up a hand as Tekker began to speak. 'And there's one more order for you. Nobody else is to know. You must tell nobody. This is my affair. Mine!'

'But if we found somebody like us who could do it,' said Tekker. 'Somebody older, I mean. They could help.'

'Worse! Can you not see, boy, what I am trying to tell you? There are dangers everywhere. And not only to you. If you blunder over there and make one false move, Stella will die!'

9
·
Wreckage

'You ought to tell somebody,' said Dan. 'It's not the kind of thing you keep to yourself. Not when an old man buries his flying helmet for you to find then lures a couple of kids back to his house. You've got to be careful.'

They were sitting on fruit boxes in the orchard shed. Tekker kicked one. 'Not so much of the kids,' he said.

Kit glowered at her brother. 'I wish we'd never told you. Mr Welbeck told us not to say anything.'

Tekker said to him, 'It's only because you know a bit already.' Then, without looking at Kit, he went on, 'Anyway, I did think I'd try the story out on someone else, so I sort of got around to it with my Dad last night.' He sensed Kit stiffen. 'But all they could talk about was my battered face.'

'Not a pretty sight,' said Dan.

'I thought I'd get my Dad to take a walk out there without telling him anything, and then we'd sort of drop in on John Welbeck and something might happen. But he only went as far as the pub.'

'Good!' said Kit.

'So I've given up the idea.' He grinned at her but it made his face throb. 'It's us or nobody.'

Dan stood up and thrust his hands deep into his trouser pockets, hunching his shoulders forward and beaming his glasses towards them. 'So,' he said, and he looked exactly like a teacher. 'You thought it best to come and tell me. Well I don't blame you two kids. I *am* older and I have got a sense of responsibility. So we'll go and sort this out once and for all.'

'Responsibility?' said Tekker. 'You?' But secretly he was relieved. 'Lead the way, Big Brother.' He winked at Kit behind Dan's back, but it made him wince.

'Serves you right,' she said, but she also was not sorry to have Dan with them when they left the shed and headed for John Welbeck's cottage. They knocked and waited, but there was no response.

'Dead or gone shopping,' said Dan. 'Oh well, let's go and have a look at your red desert.'

They went as far as the gate with him but then hung back as he turned towards the bridge. 'Scared?' he said. 'Daren't you go over there?'

'I dare.' Tekker strode forward. 'And I will, but I'm not going to make anything happen, if that's what you expect.'

'Nor me,' said Kit.

'The younger generation!' Dan clicked his tongue and turned his eyes to heaven. 'You really do need protecting from mad old men.'

They crossed the bridge, and Dan kept going, knowing they were reluctant. The orchards fell behind, and they were out under the wide sky between fields of sugar beet.

'It *is* a desert,' said Dan. 'So dull it's unbelievable.'

But Kit had not heard him. She had stopped and was pointing at something ahead. 'It's still there!' she said. There was a low hedge, and above it a lattice work of struts pointed at the sky. 'It's the aeroplane!'

'Well I'll be damned!' Dan, still their elder, allowed himself to be surprised. 'After all these years.'

He began to run, but Kit and Tekker had learned caution. They searched the skyline and the land between for signs of a change. Only when they saw that the green remained green did they go forward.

Dan had already crossed the dyke and gone through a gap in the hedge when they drew level with the wreck. It lay in a bed of nettles in an uncultivated corner, and Dan was beating a path towards the brown struts. He was shouting something, and even before they reached him he had climbed up among the spars, and sat there, looking down at them.

'Some aeroplane!' he shouted. 'Some Bristol Scout!' He kicked at one of the struts. It was iron, and flakes of rust fell off. 'It's a reaper!' He kicked again and it shook. 'It's an ancient old reaper.'

And they saw its sail arms and its cranks. It was useless iron left to fall apart in the corner of the field. They stood where they were, shamefaced, waiting for Dan to crow again. But quite suddenly the pleasure left his face and he began to slide from his perch.

'Oh my God!' He had reached the ground, but stood still as though afraid of something in front of him. They ran forward, but before they reached him they saw what it was. Stretched out on the ground, one side of his face pressed to the earth, lay John Welbeck.

10

•

Bog Oak

'He's dead, isn't he?'

Tekker heard Dan but did not reply. He noticed many things in the same instant. He felt the sting of nettles through his jeans and saw that Kit had tried to pull her skirt to protect her legs. He saw the thin mesh of veins under the old man's pale skin and did not want to touch him.

Dan had picked up John Welbeck's stick, but Kit had her head bent over the open mouth.

'He's breathing,' she said, and began to fumble at his tie.

'Let me do it,' said Tekker. The bristles on the old man's chin rasped the back of his hand but he got the tie loose. Kit, rubbing the knotted hand, looked up at Dan.

'Run and fetch someone,' she said. 'Get an ambulance.'

Dan stood where he was. He had gone very pale.

'If you won't, I will.' She began to get to her feet, but Tekker held her wrist. John Welbeck stirred, and together they turned him so that he lay on his back.

They could see the eyes moving behind closed eyelids, and suddenly his chest rose and fell and his voice came faintly on his breath. 'No ambulance.' More air shuddered into him. 'I'm not going in any ambulance.' His eyelids trembled open. For several seconds his eyes were vague but the old sharpness struggled to return and he began to push himself upright. 'Just dropped off for a minute,' he said. 'Having a nap.'

'You picked a funny spot for it,' said Tekker.

'When you're as old as I am anywhere will do.' He snorted and managed to sit up. 'Where's my blasted stick?' Dan came forward and handed it to him. He grasped it and clambered to his feet, swatting their hands away as they tried to help. But when he was upright, he had to rest, leaning heavily.

'How long have you been there?' Tekker asked.

John Welbeck ignored him. 'My damned tie's come undone.' He would not move until he had straightened it and then he began to walk away, but staggered and only Tekker prevented him falling. 'Ground's very uneven.' He was still grumbling about it when they reached the road, but he kept one arm on Tekker's shoulder as though he had merely forgotten to lift it away.

Dan was still shaken by the sight of the old man lying like a corpse, and wanted to redeem himself. He picked up the overcoat that lay among the nettles and followed.

On the bridge, John Welbeck stopped abruptly and stood free of Tekker. They all turned with him to look back. A few houses, far apart, dotted the flat land like drowsy insects resting on shimmering water. He grunted. 'Looks peaceful,' he said. 'Don't let it fool you.'

He turned his back on the plain and began descending the slope to his cottage, but once again he swayed and did not object when Tekker and Kit walked close to him on either side. By the time they got to the back door he was breathless and trembling too much to get the key into the lock. Annoyed with himself, he handed it to Tekker and then pushed past him when the door opened and let himself fall into one of the deep chairs beside the dead fire. His face was pinched and blue around the nose and cheekbones, but he shook his head when Kit suggested a doctor, and he sent Tekker into the front room to fetch the whisky decanter and a glass. His hand shook as he drank and he was aware of them looking down at him. 'Don't worry,' he said, 'I've never spilled a drop.'

'I'll bet.' Dan was beginning to recover.

John Welbeck's eyes rested on him. 'Is that what you think? That I was lying out there drunk?'

Dan shrugged.

'Can't blame you.' He put his glass down and began to push himself to his feet but thought better of it and remained seated. His eyelids flickered and his chest heaved. He seemed to want to go to sleep, but he roused himself. 'Before you go, let me just say one thing – to you two.' He spoke only to Kit and Tekker. 'It's out there, as you say. I tried your trick and found it. But for a second only.'

'What happened?' said Kit.

'I passed out.' He despised himself for it. 'Too much for an ancient man. It took a plane crash to put me through before, and now I am too old. I knew it, but I had to see what I would find. My Bristol Scout was there, but burnt out, totally. Like me.' He managed the edge of a smile. 'But there's nothing else. Not even the coat.'

'What coat?' said Dan. The old man waved away the question, but Dan pushed himself forward. 'This one?'

He had the overcoat on his arm, and as he held it out he noticed for the first time that it was leather, and stiff. He laid it over John Welbeck's knees.

'It was on the ground beside you,' said Dan. 'Under your arm.'

But the old man was not listening. With feverish hands he was thrusting into the pockets, pulling out torn linings, cracking the hardened leather, forcing open every crevice, and finally lifting the coat and shaking it. Dust and rotten cloth were all that fell free.

'It's gone.' John Welbeck lay back, and exhaustion seemed to whittle him to the bone. His voice was thin. 'Maybe it was never there. I've lost it.'

Questions began to spring from Dan, but went unanswered. John Welbeck's eyes were closed.

It was Kit who took charge. 'We'll go now,' she said, but before they left she poured another whisky and put the glass into his hand. He managed one faint, mild smile, and nodded.

Dan was himself again, and once they were outside he demanded answers. 'Can somebody explain what all this is about? Just what is it the old maniac has lost?'

'Not that it's any of your business,' said Kit, 'but it was just something his girl-friend had given him.'

'Must have been valuable to make all that fuss about it.'

'Just a piece of black wood,' said Tekker. 'Nothing for you to get excited about. Bog oak.'

Dan's laugh exploded. 'Bit of wood! Why didn't you say?' He strode ahead of them towards the gate, and whenever they tried to ask a question he said, 'Bog oak!' and laughed.

They had to go with him, and he knew it. He led them back across the bridge and out over the fen. The rusting reaper made him laugh again.

'Here's your Bristol Scout,' he said to Tekker, waving an arm towards it as he went around the bed of nettles. 'And here's your bog oak.' He stopped and picked something up. A black disc covered his palm. 'Just a bit of wood. It was under the coat.'

Tekker held out his hand, but Dan backed away.

'Oh no,' he said. 'If anybody gives this to the cranky old devil it's going to be me. Bit of bog oak – big deal.' There was a lofty smile on his face as he looked down and turned it over in his hand.

It was then that the red glare came. It caught him with
its full force. It seemed to bloom in his hand and spread
outwards in shock waves like a silent explosion. Within
the time it took him to raise his eyes it had reached the
horizon. He spun. The heat of the desert scorched his
skin.

'That glare again!' He brushed his face with his arm,
thinking he would clear the dazzle and see what caused it.
'It's got to be a flare. Must come from planes.' He scan-
ned the skyline, shading his eyes, and suddenly he was
pointing. 'There they are. Look!'

Kit came out of her daze. Tekker was already looking to
where Dan pointed. The scatter of boulders was there,
but beyond them, hanging in the deep purple of the sky,
were two black dots.

'That's them,' said Dan. 'They've got a new kind of
weapon. Searchlights or something that turns everything
red. Even all this sugar beet.' He ran out into the red
sand, kicking it ridges, believing it was rows of beet.

'Come back!' Kit started out after him, but Tekker held
her back. He was listening for engines. If he heard planes,
Dan might be right. But the desert was silent, and behind
them, where the reaper had been, the wreckage was a
Bristol Scout.

Dan was some distance from them. He stooped and
picked up a handful of sand. 'Bare earth out here,' he said.
Then he looked at the sky. 'And they don't look like any
planes I've ever seen.' Then he turned and shouted,
'They're birds!'

The dots were larger and they wavered in the sky. They
came on slowly beating wings, but Dan had lost interest
in them. He was wandering back, turning his head from
side to side, trying to work out what was happening.

Behind them, the slowness of the wingbeats was no
measure of the speed the birds were flying. They were

coming fast. Already they were larger than herons, and black. They dipped in the purple sky and swung low over the boulders. It was then that their true size was shown.

'Dan!' Kit's yell reached him. 'Run!'

He looked back. The wings, wider than houses, stretched out over the boulders like a line of black waves rising and falling along a beach.

Running was too late, but he tried. He was scurrying like a mouse when the sobbing of the wingbeats overtook him. He jinked sideways and ran off at an angle, but he only made it easier for the birds. One dipped a wingtip, and a black body as big as a boat slewed to cut him off. It dipped and raised a storm of sand. Dan was hidden.

Kit shouted his name and sprang forward, but Tekker caught her wrist and spun her. It was too late to help. The other bird, skimming the ground, swept their way.

Their only hope was the rocks. The bird angled as they turned to run in front of it. They heard its wings sigh and roar as it raced them. The rocks were still ahead when its shadow engulfed them in a black cave and a pulse of hard air flattened them. Then it was over and beyond, and turning to come back. They got to their feet, winded, and scrambled on. One rock was near. They flung themselves beside it as the bird came again. It hauled itself up short of the rocks, its wings battering the air to hold itself steady before it dropped.

But no talons came down. No beak gaped. And its wings were not bird's wings. They were leathery; huge sails of black leather, scooping air, then spreading in a glide to let a scarred keel grate in the sand. It was a flying machine.

It slid, rocking to a stop, and slowly tilted to rest on one wingtip. They searched its length for a sign of life. Nothing. There was a hump where the wings joined the body, and in front of that it was shaped liked an open boat with the front cut off. They could see into its hollow interior, and everything was still. It was a dead, hollow shell.

And then the hump between the wings stirred. It seemed to be furred like a bee's back, but the fur stiffened into a ridge and lifted. Beneath it, a pale patch they had taken for part of the structure rose with it. Blank eyes, like an insect's, gazed at them from a horse's skull and long limbs jerked through the open front to step on to the sand.

They spun and found a narrow gap in the rocks. They pushed through. There was a space of rippled sand and no way out. The boulders made walls to trap them.

They leapt and tried to climb, but there were no hand-holds and they slid helplessly and sprawled. Together, they twisted their backs to the burning rock.

The Horsehead stood in the gap, its arms raised and the bristles on the crown of its skull rippling.

11
·
Rags in a Doorway

The Horsehead's ragged snout dipped as it swayed towards them. The rock pressed into their backs, but Tekker had both arms up, ready to lash out.

The bony head fluttered. Behind it the sky had turned pale green. The spindly arms reached and Tekker thrashed once, but made no contact. The raised arms did not come down. There was a dank and musty smell that was not the burnt, dry air of the desert. And the Horsehead stood stockstill.

Kit understood before Tekker. She saw the rag hanging from the nail beside the doorway, and beyond it, through panes of broken, dusty glass, the thin branches of a dead tree which caught the breeze and flickered across the sky. They were the Horsehead's arms; its skull was the rag.

She tugged at Tekker, and very gradually his fighter's crouch relaxed.

'It's all right.' She watched him shake himself free of the desert. 'We've come back.'

'But where are we?' He moved forward cautiously. They were in a greenhouse. It was old and derelict. One corner had completely caved in and the door was permanently jammed open against the earth floor.

'I know where,' she said. 'Doubledyke. We've come all the way to the farm.'

Doubledyke Farm was deep in the fens where the road

petered out. Through the doorway they could see the roof of the farmhouse.

'Always the same.' Tekker went to the doorway and tore down the rag. Jagged moth holes still made dead eyes, and it was as stiff and brittle as thin bone. 'When you get right to the point, it always turns out to be something else.'

'Thank goodness,' she said.

'I know, but . . .' He threw the rag on the floor. 'Oh I don't know . . . Just when you think you're getting somewhere.'

'Anyone would think you weren't scared. I was. I'm glad it's just imagination.'

'Funny sort of imagination if we both saw the same thing together. Must be pretty strong.' The new thought made Kit struggle not to shiver. She kept her eyes away from him as she said, 'You don't think we're going mad, do you?'

'If we are, so is Dan.' The idea amused him. 'Mad Dan, your brother. Where is he, anyway?'

'I don't like it in here. I want to go home.'

'We'll find him sitting on the bridge, laughing at us.' He kicked at the rag. 'It's all low-flying aeroplanes and flares with him.'

'Well, it very well might be.' She had lost patience. 'I hope it is.' She went out ahead of him.

The farm was quiet, and nobody saw them leave. They had come further than they realized, and they hurried, expecting all the time to catch sight of Dan, but the road was empty and so was the bridge.

Kit's anxiety grew and she would not stop at John Welbeck's house but broke into a trot with Tekker keeping pace beside her.

'Suppose it caught him,' she said. 'Suppose he didn't get back.'

'If we did, so did he. And he'll have a theory for it. He'll say we've been hypnotized, bet you what you like. And he'll blame me for it.'

'None of this would have happened if it wasn't for you!'

She refused to listen to anything else he said, and her face was still clouded with worry as they went up the drive and around the corner of the house. But then she pulled up, sagging suddenly with relief. Through the open kitchen door they could see Dan.

Tekker went forward. 'I knew we'd find you here,' he said. 'You fooled your sister, though.'

Dan, sitting very upright, said nothing.

'Tell us what you saw when the flares came,' said Tekker. 'That is, if you admit you saw anything at all.'

Dan did not even blink, and Tekker began to find it unnerving.

'All right,' he said. 'You win. We imagined it all.' Dan did not stir, and he added lamely, 'It's a bit of a relief, to tell you the truth.'

He stepped into the kitchen, and for the first time saw Kit's mother. She was a large, plump woman, always ready to joke with him.

He grinned at her. 'I think I've offended your son, Mrs Huntley. Old Dan's angry with me.'

She was sitting at the table with both plump arms resting on it and her hands clenched in front of her. She did not seem to hear him. Her gaze was fixed on Dan and she was biting her bottom lip as though to prevent herself bursting into tears. Suddenly she turned on him.

'What have you done?' she cried. 'Why is he like this?'

Kit pushed past them both and went to stand beside her brother. Tekker heard the fluttery panic of her breathing, and his stomach went cold. Dan had not blinked nor stirred since they came into the room. The skin of his face was taut, and so smooth and pale it was inhuman. The spikes of his hair were unnatural and touched his forehead like a wig.

'He's been like this ever since he came home,' said his mother. 'He won't talk!' Almost crying, she beat her clenched hands on the table. 'Dan! What's happened to you? Why are you like this?'

He was so like a figure in a shop window that Tekker felt a touch would topple him stiffly to the floor. Only his hands looked natural. One was spread out on his thigh; the other, resting on his knee, was clenched.

Tekker wanted to touch him. That would bring old Dan back. He took a step forward, and as he did so a bird flew down into the yard behind him. He heard the quick pulse of its wings as the sunlight, streaming through the open door, was broken by its fluttering shadow. At that instant Dan changed. He focused suddenly on something beyond Tekker's back and his mouth opened. His breath came in a sharp snort, and the terror in his face made Tekker spin to see what was behind him.

A crow, its black wings glistening and spread wide, was digging its bill into the gravel.

Dan's chair clattered to the floor and he was stumbling backwards. Only the wall prevented him falling, and he slid along it until the corner of a cupboard stopped him.

His mouth opened as though he was about to cry out, but no sound came. One arm came up to cover his stomach, and he held out his other hand, still clenched, as though to offer something.

His fingers uncurled. In his palm lay the black disc of bog oak.

12

.

A Pretty Face

'You've gone too far this time.'

Kit's mother sat at one end of the sofa in a room at the front of the house. She held herself upright as though worse disaster would strike if she leant back. They could hear the doctor moving in Dan's bedroom overhead.

'I'm sorry, Mum,' said Kit.

'It's too late to be sorry.'

Tekker had always liked Kit's mother, but now that her son was ill her face had hardened and her eyes were black and cold. He was afraid of her but he had to speak.

'I started it.' His voice gave out and he had to clear his throat. 'It's not Kit's fault.'

The eyes that were turned on him were dead. She said nothing.

'Dan will be all right soon, Mrs Huntley.'

'You *know* that, do you?' She pressed her lips together bitterly. 'You're cleverer than the doctor, are you? You terrorize my son so that his mind has gone, and you say he'll be all right!'

Tekker backed out of the room, pushed by the hard glare of her eyes. He had told everything – almost all of it – when the doctor had questioned them, but the doctor had grunted impatiently and took in only as much as he wanted to. Then there had been talk, which excluded him, of hysteria, of something getting out of hand, and

Dan having some sort of weakness in his body that nobody suspected.

Tekker stood in the sun outside but it did not warm him. He was at the side door looking blankly at the doctor's car parked at the front and hearing, somewhere within the house, the jangle as the telephone was replaced on its cradle. A long silence, and then light footsteps on the kitchen floor. Kit stood at the door, her face so pale it seemed to lack all features except eyes.

'They're not sure what's wrong.' Her voice was very small.

'Isn't it . . .' He had to force himself to say it. 'Is it his heart?'

'They're not sure. They might have to take him to hospital.'

There was more movement inside the house and, out of their sight, the front door opened and the doctor came out, promising he would be back within an hour with something he needed.

'Wait a minute, Kit.' Tekker did not want her to go back indoors. She paused, and he searched his mind for something to keep her. 'Can't we do something for him?'

'What?' She was impatient.

He had no idea. He clenched his fists and realized he was holding something. 'There's always this,' he said. He held out the black disc he had prised from Dan's fingers.

'I don't want to touch it.'

'But it might help.'

'How?'

'I don't know, Kit. But it really is what old John Welbeck was looking for, and nothing happened to Dan until he found it.'

'I wish he'd never set eyes on it!'

He turned it over in his hand. 'It's got a picture scratched on it. Just like he said.'

He held it out and, in spite of herself, she looked at the black disc. Thin lines were scratched on its surface. At first they seemed no more than the grain of the ancient wood, but then the mesh of tiny wrinkles took shape. Still without touching it, she looked closer. It was a landscape. There was a flat, low skyline, and in the middle distance, across a plain, there was what seemed to be a palace, or a city of many buildings on a hill with a single tower reaching high into the sky.

'I just thought, Kit, that if we went to see John Welbeck he might say something that could help old Dan.'

The eyes she turned on him were resentful, blaming him for all that had happened.

'It wouldn't do any harm.' He felt skinned to the bone. 'We've got to do something.'

She said nothing until he took hold of her hand and began to tug her. Then she said, 'This has got to be the last time.'

'It will be.'

It was a relief to be doing something, and it was also necessary. They had forgotten until they rounded the corner of John Welbeck's house in what state they had left him. The back door was ajar and they pushed it open as they knocked to see him still sitting in the same chair. His eyes were misty, as though he had been sleeping and, for a while, he was confused.

The kettle over the dead fire was cold, but Kit had noticed the little kitchen leading off his sitting-room, and she found a stove and an electric kettle and she made him tea. She put whisky in it, and was going to hold it for him as he drank, but he brushed her away. Nevertheless, he had to hold the cup in both hands.

'Damn it,' he said. 'I'm about ready for the scrapyard.'

'Not yet awhile.' Tekker tried to talk the old man's

nguage. 'You've got something to do first.' He held out
e black disc.

Kit had moved forward to take the cup, sure that he
ould snatch at the black wood, but the old man sat quite
ill. 'So you've got it.' He leant down to put his cup in the
earth.

'It was under the coat,' said Tekker. 'Near the crash.'

John Welbeck nodded slowly. Still he did not reach for
e disc, but his eyes did not leave it. 'And what happened?'

'Dan.' Kit started forward. 'Please you've got to help,
Mr Welbeck. Dan had it and they came and hurt him.'

'I see.'

'He's pretty bad,' said Tekker.

John Welbeck stared at the disc. They could hear their
own breathing as, very slowly, he began to advance one
and towards it. He had reached only midway when he
opped, and his eyes switched suddenly to the window. He
ad heard something. They listened with him. After a
oment they heard the front gate click.

'Visitor,' he grunted. 'Just as I expected.' Suddenly he
rust himself to his feet. 'Don't want you two here. This
ay.' His voice had its old command, and he ushered them
o a door behind his chair. 'In there and stay quiet.'

They went through into the narrow hall. There was a
ttle window in the door designed to let light into the dark
assage, but it was covered by a pair of curtains. He parted
em slightly so that they could see into the room. 'Watch
nd listen. On no account come out.' He pulled the door to,
aving it just a crack open, and they saw him hobble
uickly back to his chair.

Behind them the front door rattled as someone tried it,
nd they jumped when a loud knock echoed in the dim
orridor. John Welbeck made no attempt to answer it. The
nock came again. There was an impatient pause, and then
ootsteps went off along the side of the house.

They were peering through the gap in the curtain when there was a quick rap on the back door, and almost immediately the latch rattled and it was pushed open.

Fat white fingers gripped the edge and held the door motionless. Ma Grist was solid. It showed in the tightness of the brown coat she wore in spite of the sun, and there was a bulge of fat under the single straps of her shoes. She blocked out the light, and even behind their door they wanted to shrink back. But then she smiled. The grim line of the mouth they had seen in the dark garden did not exist. It had vanished, and in its place there was sweetness and round cheeks, and a small button of a nose. Her face had a plump prettiness that was not spoiled by the small, round glasses she wore nor the old-fashioned brown hat with a brim that put a shadow across her brow.

'Well now.' Even in two words they could hear the warmth in her voice, and the kindliness. Her hand fell from the latch and she stepped further into the room. 'They tell me you haven't been too well, John, so I thought I'd just step by. No, there's no need to get up. Sit you down.'

She took another half step and raised a hand as though she was going to rest it on his shoulder, but he had already pushed himself to his feet.

'Madam,' he said, and his voice and the way he bowed to her were both so stiff that Kit winced. He was making a mistake. Ma Grist was nice. They had all been wrong. Even now the plump face was beaming in spite of his rudeness. She understood awkward old men.

'I see you've made yourself a cup of tea,' she said, and chuckled, adding hastily, 'Not that I was hinting that' what I'd come by for, John. I'm just relieved to see you can get it for yourself. They've been telling me such things about you.'

'They?' He snapped out the question.

'My friends, John.' She was looking around her, cradling one hand in the other as though finding it difficult not to bustle around the room and do things for him. 'My word, but you do seem to be nice and cosy here.'

'And will remain so, Madam. Your friends cannot get in here.'

'Ever such a cosy, warm little room. That's right, sit down and rest your legs.'

John Welbeck had seated himself more quickly than he would have wished. His weakness was showing. He was breathless, partly with anger. 'I can order you out!'

He had gone mad. Kit, biting a thumbnail, saw Tekker's mouth open as though he could feel the pain that the savage old man must be inflicting on the motherly face that still smiled at him.

'You wouldn't do that to me, John.' Her voice was soft, covering the hurt she must feel. 'You couldn't tell me to go.'

'I could. And I would. There's enough of Stella left in me to do it. Quite enough.'

As he uttered the name of her sister she sighed, shaking her head. 'Poor Stella,' she said. 'Poor Stella.'

Silence fell, and they saw the knobbed knuckles of the old man's hand working as he gripped the arm of his chair. When he spoke he struggled to keep his voice level. 'She is not poor Stella. Not to you. You have her. Out there.' His head nodded towards the window and the fens beyond. 'In the place she showed me. You keep her there. But you cannot finish us. We are still too strong.'

'Finish you? Oh, John, you don't know what you say. Poor Stella's gone. Gone for good. You know that.' She tilted her head forward, and her face was hidden.

'Listen!' His bark startled her and the hatpin that skewered the brown hat to the grey hair glinted as her head jerked up. 'Listen to every word I say. You have her.

And you have me – almost. But other people know of you now. Youngsters. And they must not be harmed.'

He was leaning forward angrily, but she still answered him softly, 'Oh John, John, is it necessary to be like this?'

'Youngsters. Are you listening?' Behind the door their flesh crawled. He was talking directly to them. 'They found their way into that country out there. To the fringes, but no further. You frightened them away; you and your friends. It was easy for you. Their powers were slight. No match for yours. But they have stumbled on the one thing that makes a difference.'

His voice had become far too loud. Ma Grist must realize he was talking to someone else, but her attention was fixed on the old man. Her face remained plump and pretty, but all her features seemed to have become tiny and bunched together in her pale flesh.

'Stella's disc,' he said. Only her eyes moved. Little licks of green, they slid like snails behind her glasses, left and right, before they centred on him and held steady. 'You believed I had it all these years. But you thought it was useless, all the power that Stella put into it drained away.' He shook his head. 'Wrong. It lay out there.'

She nodded. 'Until the boy Huntley found it today and picked it up. He should never have done that.' Her voice remained soft, but it was as cold as water on marble. Chill flowed outwards until the room and the corridor outside were gripped by it. 'My friends saw him, John, and tried to get it from him. He got away, but it has done him little good.'

'It got him out.'

'By chance. Any child can turn a key by chance.' She held out a hand. 'Give it to me.'

'Key?' Deliberately he sat back.

'That disc is not just a keepsake from your Stella. It's a key. You know that as well as I do.' She turned her plump hand first palm up, then palm down. 'In and out, John Welbeck. It takes anybody in and out of that land. But you are too old to use it. Give.'

'No.' He spoke curtly and reached towards his shirt pocket with such certainty that Tekker could not prevent himself glancing down. He still gripped the disc. John Welbeck was putting on an act.

'Give!' The plump fingers rippled.

'You cannot take what Stella gave to me. You have not the strength.'

Her hand drew back and was once again cradled in the other. 'Maybe not, John. But now that I know you have it I can put a curb round it.' Her eyes closed, and the tip of a pink tongue touched the corners of her mouth. 'The boy Huntley was an unbeliever, John. Only the disc made him really see. Stella got through to him and showed him the desert. Not much more.' She frowned and trembled slightly as her hands turned whiter, gripping each other as though they struggled. 'But I've taken my sister further away, John. The disc would be useless to him now. Useless to anybody like him.'

'But not to me!'

'But you already know what is out there, John. You are half way there already.'

'I shall use it.'

'Please don't be silly.' She spoke like somebody comforting a child. 'I can send my friends to see you don't get up to mischief with it.'

'They cannot enter this house. There's enough of Stella here to keep them out.'

'And you cannot leave. My friends touched the boy, remember. One touch was all it needed. He will die.'

Kit's breath was sucked in with a thin cry at the back of her throat as John Welbeck, sensing the sound, shoved back his chair and snorted, 'Stella will save him!'

The little lips were pursed and the eyes were bright, but still the voice was soft. 'She is too far away, John, and you can never reach her. You are too old. Far to old.'

His lips were tight shut but he was fighting for breath. He could hardly stand. 'Spare the boy,' he said.

She shook her head. 'People should not interfere. I'm afraid what must be, must be.'

'I have the key.' He defied her. 'I will reach her.'

She gave a tiny, dry laugh. 'She is well fenced in, John. I've seen to it over the years. Can your old bones cross the desert? Can you lower yourself down a cliff? Can you cross miles of marsh? Can you climb stairs, John? The stairs that she built? Don't blame me for the stairs.'

He was bent slightly at the hip, struggling to straighten, and once again he breathed deeply before he spoke. 'I will give you the disc for the boy's life.'

'Why should I bargain? All I have to do is wait. You cannot have much time left, John.'

He swayed slightly, almost at the end of his strength. 'The disc for the boy,' he said.

The plump face looked down at him from across the room. 'I think not,' she said. 'He has some stupid young friends, I believe. They were with him and they might have ideas. It will keep them occupied to see him fade away.'

She stood watching as gradually he sagged into his chair, unable to stand any longer. Then she said, 'You won't keep me waiting long. I doubt if you can cross the room.' She began to turn her bulk away from him, but paused. 'All hope is gone now, John. I shall call my friends to make sure you have no visitors.'

She turned her back on him and it was then that John Welbeck called up the last of his strength. He thrust himself upright.

'Go!' he yelled. 'Get out of this house!'

But his shout was not directed at Ma Grist. He had turned to the curtained door, and was urging them away. They were slow to move, and she looked back over her shoulder. He faced her and yelled again. 'Go!'

In the dim corridor they crept backwards to the door at the front of the house. There was one bolt and it was stiff. Tekker was working at it when they heard the sound.

On the back doorstep, Ma Grist had held out her hand and from her lips came a chirruping, birdlike noise as she coaxed something towards her through the trees of the garden.

13
.
At the Edge

The bolt, suddenly loosened, shot back with a click and they were outside in the blinding sunshine. The shrill chirruping from behind the house pierced their heads and they ran from it along the path and through the gate.

In the road they twisted, not knowing which way to run, but the whickering sound suddenly ceased, and footsteps coming along the side of the house drove them into cover.

Across the road there was a ditch, choked and overgrown. They plunged down its steep side, thrust themselves into the tallest reeds and crouched.

'Keep still!' Tekker whispered as the reeds trembled overhead.

The ditch was almost dry, but water seeped through its bed and into their shoes as they faced each other, listening.

The gate rattled, there was a brief silence, and then a quick shuffle, jigging like dance steps on the road above them. Silence again. Then footsteps. Going away.

They eased themselves up the bank and peered through the grass of the verge. A brown figure was plodding steadily towards the village.

At last Kit could speak. 'Oh Dan!' she said. 'Poor Dan!' She thrust herself upright. 'I'll kill her! She'll never get him!' And then she was sobbing, pushing herself away from Tekker.

Her storm made him thin and lame, and he did nothing

but watch her and the retreating figure, now almost hidden by a bend. He waited until the sobbing eased and then he said, 'There's still this, Kit.' He held out the disc.

She brushed her eyes fiercely with the back of her hand. 'Give!'

The word was Ma Grist's and he hesitated, but she snatched it and turned it over with fingers still damp with tears. 'In and out,' she said, clencing her teeth. 'In and out. I'll get into her damned desert. I'll find her sister. I'll finish her!'

Tekker looked beyond her. The brown figure was out of sight. 'When do we start?' he said.

'Now!'

Her brow was bent like an eagle's, and her ferocity stirred him into a grimace that was almost a laugh. 'Now?'

'Now!'

They went quickly towards the bridge, but they had become as cunning as hunting animals and they crouched as they neared the top of the slope to look back and down at John Welbeck's house. It was peaceful under the sun, but there was a shadow across one corner of the lawn at the back that did not belong to a tree. Whatever made it was hidden by the corner, but it guarded the door.

Tekker was about to step onto the bridge, but she prevented him.

'Hold this.' She handed the disc to him and from the pocket of her skirt she took out a purse with a drawstring top. She tipped out what money there was and gave it to him as she took back the disc and slid it into the purse. 'I've got to try something,' she said as she drew the strings tight.

'What are you doing?'

'It lay under the coat out there all those years and nothing happened. Might be best to keep it in the dark until we need it.'

'Kit's a clever kid,' he said.

'Autographs later.' She managed a tight little smile. 'Now let's go.'

They crossed the water and stopped twenty paces down from the bridge. She held out the purse and twisted it one way and then the other. They had screwed up their eyes against the blinding redness, but nothing happened. She was beginning to pull the purse open when Tekker stopped her.

'Why don't we go deeper?' he said. 'We can perhaps get further than the boulders.'

'You've got brains as well as me.'

They broke into a trot but slowed when they came to the ruined greenhouse near the farm.

'Further than this,' he said.

Some geese hissed but parted as they advanced, and when the road petered out beyond the quiet farmhouse they followed a track between two dykes. Far away, a tractor was moving over the flat land, but no sound reached them.

'We're leaving Dan behind.' Alarm caught in her throat.

He forced her into a run, and when he was sure that the boulders, invisible on the fields, were behind them, he stopped. She opened the purse and slid the disc into his hand. It was face down. He glanced at her, and when she nodded he turned it over.

They were ready for the glare, and it came, but this time with a bodily wrench that sent them both staggering. They lost their balance, thudded into something solid and slid to the ground. Hot sand was beneath them and red walls rose on every side. But above them there was open sky. Tekker was pushing himself to his feet when he realized where they were.

'We've been pushed back,' he said. Kit, still sitting on the sand, was bewildered. 'It's the last place we were in before we came out.' He pointed to a slit in the rocks through which the scarlet horizon lay under the purple sky. 'It chased us in through there.'

She got to her feet, startled, but Tekker crouched where he was. He held the disc out and turned it face down on his palm.

A ripple of light washed the redness from the walls and roofed them with greyness. Kit shrank back from the slit. It remained where it was but broadened slightly, and now it was a doorway through which she could see a farmhouse roof. They were in the ruined greenhouse.

They moved cautiously to the door. The stiff rag lay on the ground where Tekker had thrown it, and outside the geese were feeding along the verges of the road.

'Damn,' said Tekker, 'that's messed everything up. I thought we might be able to cover a lot of ground before we switched over. But we've got to go in where we came out.'

'Quick, then,' said Kit. 'We've got a long way to go.' She was biting her lip, frowning and anxious. A new thought had struck her. 'And we don't even know which way to go. And we haven't got much time!'

He turned the disc. From the gap between the boulders they looked out on a flat red page of sand on which the rocks were spaced, but each now throwing a longer shadow to mark the tilt of the sun down the sky like a thousand sun dials. One outcrop could have marked the farmhouse, but loneliness and endless heat lay all around them.

A trail of footprints made Tekker draw in his breath, until he realized they had made them themselves when they were being hunted. And there were the feathery marks of something with larger steps that had come in at the side to trap them. This second trail made him search for danger. Nothing. The sky was clear and nothing slid out of sight behind the rocks. They stepped out, not knowing where to go.

'The sun might help,' he said. 'And if that was the farmhouse, if must be that way.' He pointed beyond the outcrop, but Kit did not look. She was moving away to one side so that the rock did not block her view. The heat shimmer far away dissolved what she had seen, but then it came again and she stopped and beckoned him alongside her.

'Look!' Her finger took his gaze out to the horizon. 'See?'

The air quivered and he saw nothing. But her finger stabbed, insisting, and then through the shimmer it appeared. A pinprick of light, blue and dazzling, trembled on the horizon.

'That's it,' she said. 'That's where we've got to go.'

There was no other direction. Nothing else showed anywhere on the level horizon.

They set out, and soon they were in the open, with the rocks behind them and no shelter anywhere.

'It's the top of the world,' said Tekker. 'We're just about out in space.'

It was as though they were on a huge platform and the thought made Kit giddy. She reached for the disc he had been holding face upwards in his hand. 'Give me that. I want to try something else,' she said, and she slid it carefully into her purse, pulled the strings tight and then turned it over. They remained where they were in the desert. To turn the key and find the way out they would have to bring it out into the light.

'You're good at this, Kit,' he said.

'I've got to be.'

He nodded and took the purse from her and buttoned it into his shirt pocket. 'I can reach it quick enough,' he said, 'if anything comes.' He searched the bare, red plain. 'We'd see anything a mile away.'

'And they'd see us.' But she hardly cared. She was hot, and they had a long way to go.

They shaded their eyes as they walked and tried to make out the glittering point, but it was like hoping to see the shape of a star. Sometimes it dwindled to a burning orange, and then would flare to a whiteness that seemed to bring it closer, before it went away again to a green and blue pinprick of fire far away. All they knew was that they had to reach it.

Sometimes the sand was ribbed hard and they walked easily, but then a hidden hollow would send them sliding and they would have to labour up the far side. They came to the top of one such dip and had to rest.

'It's no closer!' she cried. 'We've been walking hours.' The sun had slid halfway down the sky and their shadows were longer, but the sand still burned her bare legs where she sat.

'Give me your shoes.' Tekker took them from her, tied the laces together and slung them with his own around his neck. It was easier to walk barefoot, but he knew they could not go on much longer. 'I wonder where we are,' he said. 'How far from the farm?'

The scatter of boulders had long since disappeared in the heat shimmer that lay like a skim of water over the land.

'I'm thirsty,' he said.

Kit could see what was in his mind. He was thinking that by simply turning the key they could find one of the cool waterways out in the fens.

'No.' She stood up. 'What if something goes wrong? And we haven't got time. There's Dan.'

They pressed on, and gradually walking became easier as their bare feet sensed that the ground was harder. Soon there was only a skim of sand over rock, but by now the burning redness was hurting not only their feet but their eyes and only occasionally did they raise their heads to look through slits of eyelids at the glittering point that led them on.

Tekker tried to moisten his lips to speak, but it was almost impossible. 'Have you noticed anything, Kit?' His voice was hoarse. She shook her head. 'I think we're climbing.'

Her head had drooped, and she had been watching the swing of her hair as she walked, but now she raised it. Something had happened to the skyline. It seemed closer. And Tekker was right: the land was sloping very gradually upwards.

They stopped and looked from left to right. 'We're climbing a hill.' The sparkling light lay beyond the crest. 'Perhaps we're nearly there.'

The thought drove them on. They walked faster, but the slope became steeper and the sand ended in slabs of glittering red rock, cracked and cut through with fissures that ran away ahead of them towards a jagged skyline.

The fissures broadened as they climbed so that the rock was split open and ribbed with wide gulleys that made them climb in single file. And the rock was too hot for the bare soles of their feet. They must have climbed further than they knew, for the air was thin and they were panting when they stopped and he handed Kit her shoes.

The rushing whistle in the air took them by surprise. It began as a sigh that had them looking towards each other, puzzled, not knowing where it came from. Then, like the slow breathing of an enormous throat, it came closer. It was on the other side of the slope.

They slithered round on the rock. Nothing showed on the skyline, but the next vast sigh was louder. They had to get out. Tekker reached for the disc, but was hindered by the shoes that were still around his neck. His hand felt the shape within his pocket, but it was too late.

Away to their left, a shape rose suddenly above the ridge. It lifted over the brow of the hill on black wings and came at them.

Tekker's hand was tangled. He was struggling to free it when Kit's arm caught him around the neck and hauled him backwards over the edge of the rock. He hit the bottom of the crevice with Kit half on top of him. His shoulder was jammed beneath him and his face was pressed against the rock so he could not see. He heard the lift of the wings and the downward thrust as the shadow crossed.

Kit saw the Horsehead. It leant forward in the front of the machine. Its limbs were spread out, and its bony snout dipped as the blank sockets searched. Then blackness. The keel skimmed the crevice and was gone in a whirlpool of air.

They separated and crouched. Tekker had the purse in his hand and was fumbling with the drawstrings as the eddies of sand and dust settled around them. He paused, listening. There was no beat of wings. The only sound was the thin singing of the rocks in the heat.

Very slowly, steadying themselves against the sides of the crevice, they eased themselves upright. The machine was already far away, no bigger than a bird above the ridge. It had missed them.

Tekker's shoulder hurt, and so did the side of his face. She saw him feel it, tenderly.

'Did I do that?' she said.

'You and Fatty Piggins. You nearly killed me pulling me down here.'

She watched him as he touched his face again, grimacing, with shoes dangling around his neck, and suddenly she could not stop herself laughing. 'Sorry,' she said, 'sorry, but you look a mess.'

'Your fault.'

'I had to do it. It might have seen us.'

The thought should have made them afraid, but they grinned at each other and then snarled like cats, face to face. They dared risk anything.

'What's next?' he said, and she pointed to the crest of the hill.

The crevice ran upwards with the slope of the rocks and it deepened and widened so that they were able to move along it side by side as they climbed to the ridge of the hill. They caught a glimpse of the far horizon and then, as they approached the top, they looked down to see what lay on the other side.

There was no slope. They jolted to a standstill, swaying. They were half a pace from the lip of a cliff so high that it put the horizon far below.

14

·

Picked Up

It was the edge of the world. The ground ceased and space yawned. The cliff fell away out of sight and they were grains on its lip. A whisper of air would send them over.

They edged backwards and sat facing each other. Their minds raced. It was impossible to go on. Stella was out of reach. Her sister had won. Then Tekker saw a different cloud cross Kit's face. Dan.

'I'm going to take another look,' he said.

He crawled up the stone until his hands were a fingernail from the rim. There was earth below, but so far away it was hazy and without detail. He lay flat and eased forward so that his head was over the edge. The drop was sheer. He turned his head to look along the cliff face. It was a wall that curved away on either side, a vast crescent that stretched its arms to hook onto the horizon far away.

Kit came up alongside him. The trembling in her arms made her movements jerky. Heights terrified her, and she looked without seeing.

'There are cracks just below,' he said. 'We might get a handhold.'

Kit shut her eyes, but in the darkness the rock seemed to tilt and she was sliding into space. Her eyes opened wide, and suddenly, far out over the hazy plain, a shaft of dazzling light exploded into the sky. She drew in her breath, fearing the blast that would follow, but the light stood there in utter silence. It was a column that reached far into the blue and then, as they shielded their eyes against it, it dissolved. It shed fragments of different colours, blues and greens and slivers of red, like a fountain falling back to earth in the sun. A moment later and it had vanished except for a turmoil of glittering light at its base and the ghost of itself against the sky.

They waited, hardly breathing, but it did not come again. Kit was the first to slither back down the slope.

'That's it!' she said. 'We saw the tip of it from right back there.' The red desert stretched out behind them to a flat horizon. 'We've got to reach it. We've got to.'

Tekker rubbed his hand backwards and forwards across the rock as he concentrated. 'We need things,' he said. 'Rope. We can't do the first bit without rope.' He did not mention the cliff, but she nodded. 'We shall have to get back home.'

'Do it, then. Quick.'

They slithered further down from the edge before he pulled open the purse and tipped the disc into her hands. The picture was uppermost. She turned it over.

Instantly the light blurred, and as it did so the red rock softened to green and seemed to whisper as it changed. A faint breeze cooled them and, as the light sharpened again, they saw that they lay half way down a bank in deep grass. The bank cut across fields in a straight line, but there was no drainage canal at its foot.

'Where are we?' he said. 'I'm lost.'

They sat up and looked around. Like rabbits in a hayfield, thought Tekker. And like rabbits they flattened themselves as a murmur from further along the bank swelled suddenly and a shadow brushed the grass, speeding towards them. There was a tremble in the earth, and a rumble as a large shape came sweeping along the top of the bank. They pressed themselves flat, hiding from the swoop. But it did not come. An engine roared and they heard wheels rattle. They raised their heads. They were on a railway embankment and a train was coming.

They crouched as the blue and yellow railcar rumbled by overhead, and then they climbed to try to get their bearings. It was very quiet in the afternoon sun. The train had dwindled to a little yellow cabin going further and further away and the only sound came from the grasshoppers invisibly busy on the bank. A heat haze burned the landscape to liquid and made the far horizon as blue as the sea. Only in one place was there anything large enough to loom over its edge. The towers of Ely Cathedral, the hub of the whole huge disc, pointed bluntly at the sky. But, closer, there was a low island of trees and roofs.

'That must be Manea,' said Tekker. He had biked there when he went fishing at Welches Dam, where three drains joined. He looked to see if he could find the road where it should cross the line. A car glinted up the slope towards the crossing. 'It's Manea all right. We've come a long way.'

Kit was already walking along the line, stepping from sleeper to sleeper.

'Where are you going?' he called. 'That's not the way back.'

'Yes it is, if we get a lift.'

He went with her, and when they came nearer the crossing they slid down the bank to avoid the signalman in his box, and picked up the road further along. Neither had ever tried hitchhiking, and stood uncertainly by the verge. Two cars drove by, ignoring their vague signals, then Kit took a pace out into the road.

'It's for Dan,' she said. 'We've got to get help.' She

waved her arms wildly over her head, and a truck, bearing
down on them, had to pull out and brake. They ran up to
the cab.

'What the hell you trying to do?' The driver had the
door half open. 'Get killed?'

'We shall get in a row if we don't get home.' Kit stood
below and looked up into his red face.

'Bloody kids!' The man was on the verge of slamming
the door when he looked down at her again. Tekker saw
her. She was gazing up as wide-eyed as a kitten; just
standing there, defying the man to be cruel. It was
blatant, and Tekker winced, but the man weakened. 'All
right,' he said. 'I'll do it this time.' He watched them as
they squeezed into the other seat, and his anger had not
been entirely overcome. 'Don't lean on that door,' he said,
'or you might fall out and that'll drop me right in it.
Bloody kids.'

As they rattled along the straight road to the village,
Kit told the man a long story about how they had gone
out walking and got lost.

'Lost?' he said. 'Out here? You can't get lost out here.
There's nowhere to get lost in.'

'We managed it,' said Kit, and turned her eyes on him.
'We're pretty good at it.'

He looked at her suspiciously, and then watched the
road. 'I don't know who's taking who for a ride round
here,' he said, but he took them as far as the centre of the
village before putting them down.

'Thanks very much,' they called from the roadside.

He put the lorry in gear. 'Bloody kids,' he said.

15

·

The Cliff

Dan lay upstairs. The whole house was trapped in a silence so deep it seemed dead, but every so often there would be a flurry of footsteps along the hall or the landing and panic seemed to flutter everywhere.

Kit found her father in the kitchen. He was getting tea ready while her mother stayed at Dan's bedside.

'We're not leaving him.' He had a thin, leathery face and his big hands moved slowly, placing cups and plates on the table. 'The doctor's coming back to have another look at him.' He turned to Kit, who had Tekker standing behind her, and the corners of his eyes wrinkled as he tried to smile, but the bleakness could not be disguised. 'He's no worse,' he said.

'I'm going to see him.' She tugged Tekker with her, brushing past her father.

It was a much bigger house than Tekker's and he had never been upstairs. When she pushed at Dan's bedroom door it opened into a hollow, greenish light in which the bed seemed very small, and the figure in it even smaller. The peaceful, pale face, eyes closed, did not look like Dan. His mother sat at the bedside looking at him, and barely turned to see them come into the room.

'How is he?' Kit's whisper trembled so feebly Tekker could barely hear it.

Her mother smoothed the sheet and did not answer.

'Oh, Mum!' Kit went closer, and her mother put an arm around her waist. They stayed like that, heads together, and Dan's marble face ignored them.

It was the first time Tekker had seen Dan's room. It was not like his own. The furniture was spaced out widely, and it was neat. Dan's desk in the corner had a single poster pinned squarely above it, a pattern of wheels advertising a science museum, and the clothes he had last worn were folded on the chair. Only the training shoes on the floor seemed human. They were scuffed and worn, and were down at heel and had bulged to the shape of Dan's feet. He was a fierce footballer.

Suddenly the thought of Dan running, sliding into a tackle, fighting for the ball, made Tekker move. He had to get him out of bed, and there was only one way. He grasped Kit's wrist and tugged her gently until her mother released her and then he drew her to the door.

On the landing he whispered urgently and she nodded. Her eyes were wet and she wiped them, but she was listening. When he had finished they both moved quickly.

He left her and rode home. He had no appetite, but tea was ready and he forced himself to eat as his mother questioned him about Dan. When he thought he had pacified her, he went to his room, tipped out the books that were still in his school haversack, and put in whatever he thought might be needed. He told them, as he left the house, he was taking something to amuse Dan.

Kit was waiting. She had changed her dress for jeans and a shirt, and she led him to the shed where her father kept his tractor. There was a coil of rope tossed over a beam, and Tekker pulled it down and got it into his haversack.

He did not ask if she was scared at what they were going to do, but he wanted to be sure that nobody would miss her.

'They won't.' She shook her head. 'I think they want me out of the way. The doctor's coming again.'

She had turned her back and was on her bicycle, not wanting to talk any more about Dan.

It was early evening, still teatime for many people, and there was a lull in the traffic. They kept to the main road and cycled fast through the hot air that made the tarmac ahead of them quiver like water. Near the railway crossing, they hid their bikes in the grass of the ditch at the roadside and made their way along the edge of a wheatfield to the foot of the railway embankment where they were out of sight of the signal box. The flattened grass showed the place where they had climbed.

'We need the exact spot,' said Tekker, 'then we shan't be thrown about when it happens.'

They found the place half-way up the bank. No trains were coming and they crouched and turned the disc. The fields flooded with red and the road vanished. All sound ceased. No grasshoppers sang and even the sigh of the grass had gone. The silence deadened Tekker's voice. 'I'll go first.'

The shirt pocket no longer seemed safe so he put the disc in its purse deep in his jeans pocket, and then he took the rope from the haversack and spread it on the sand. It was worn and supple, but strong. He put it twice around his waist and tied a bowline. He did the same for Kit, and then settled the haversack between his shoulders. He grinned. 'At least I feel like a mountain climber,' he said. 'All I've got to do is act like one.'

'And me.' She tried to moisten her lips, but her mouth was too dry. 'What do I do?'

'Stop me falling. I'll show you.' He crawled into the crevice between the rocks and worked his way up the slope. Emptiness yawned ahead of him but he refused to let his eyes see it. He concentrated on the rock. It was

split, and in places it jutted out in blunt fingers. None of
them was exactly what he wanted, but near the edge there
was a clumsy fist which took a full turn of the rope. It was
only then that he looked down. The sheer drop sucked at
him. He fought it and hung his head over the edge, concentrating on the face of the rock. It was fissured. There
were cracks that would hold feet and hands. He reached
over and tested an outcrop. Nothing crumbled.

He slithered back. 'Me first,' he said. 'If there's nothing
coming.'

She had forgotten everything except the cliff but, as
they moved together towards the edge, they searched the
skyline. The vast crescent of the precipice curved away
to vanish on the horizon, and the sun, slanting down the
sky, caught drifting mist and made golden layers far
below. And then, from the centre of the plain, it came
again. A towering column of light lifted suddenly to the
tip of the sky in one blinding streak that made them
crouch and cling and again wait for the blast. But in an
instant it had vanished and no sound came. All that
remained was the glittering hill at its base. They strained
their eyes but could see no detail in the hill's rippling
lights, and the amber haze on the valley floor crept higher
to cover it.

'It's almost gone,' she whispered, but Tekker had seen
something move. He nudged her without speaking, and
pointed.

Far away to their left a dark speck lifted from the cliff
and began to drift towards the centre. As they watched
another joined it. More followed and suddenly, away to
their right, a great shape spread its wings and soared from
the rim of the cliff.

They shrank further back into the crevice, and a clatter
of wings told them another had been poised even closer.
They waited, perspiration trickling on their necks, but

the wingbeats faded and no more came. The dots were far away.

'Lucky,' he said softly. 'We might have come through right next to one of them.'

'Where was it?'

'It was resting I should think. On the edge.' He squinted at the sun. 'It's going to be dark before long. They're being called in.'

'Why?'

'They've been out on patrol, I reckon.' He forced a grin. 'Making sure nobody gets through. But it didn't work, did it? They didn't spot us.'

'There's still the cliff.'

'Easy,' he said. 'I went up the church tower once, when they were repairing it, and I wasn't even giddy.'

'I don't believe you, Tekker Begdale.'

'Betty Sutton did.'

'Her! Why do you want to mention her right in the middle of all this?'

'Makes you mad, does it?'

'So do you.'

Angrily, she was coiling the rope in her hand as she spoke.

'You look like an expert,' he said.

'Good as you, any day.'

'Right, then. You go first.'

'I will.' Her eyes were dark with anger, and she kept them that way. Better to be angry than afraid. 'Keep that rope tight.'

She moved towards the edge and lay flat on her stomach, pushing herself backwards, legs first. He leant back on the rope, holding it tight.

Emptiness yawned at her back. She spread her arms wide and laid her cheek against the rock as her feet kicked at the cliff face. The toe of one shoe scratched, slipped, then found a crevice. Then the other.

He saw her stop moving. 'I've got you,' he said.

She eased back an inch. Her toes held. Another inch and her weight was bearing down.

'Ease out a bit.' Her words came in a gasp.

He paid out the rope, at the same time reaching to hold her hand but she needed it for herself and slid it away clinging to the rock edge.

Feet. Look no further than your feet. She instructed herself as she moved. She jammed one hand into a jagged crack, pulled one toe from its crevice and slid it inches further down the cliff. Her heart was pounding as though it was trying to jerk her into space. There was a tiny ledge no more than an inch wide. It would have to do. She put her foot sideways on it, and moved the other hand from the cliff edge to where, with her fingertips, she could just cling to the roughness of the rock.

She rested, getting her breath. She was an arm's length down from the edge, spreadeagled on the cliff face. There was slackness in the rope. Only her toes and fingers held her. A skin's thickness kept her from falling.

She was muttering to herself over and over, 'I can do it, I can do it,' as though the words were glue and if she stopped she would fall.

She searched for the next foothold and crabbed down another few inches. Then she had to rest, her muscles trembling with the strain.

'Kit.'

His head, jutting out from the edge above, seemed suddenly to be moving against the blue sky and giddiness made the cliff face tilt. She shut her eyes and felt it sway. She would fall away. Space would gulp her. Nothing could stop it.

Then his voice reached her again. 'It looks a bit easier just to your right.'

'Shut up!' she cried. 'I can't reach it! I can't! I can't!' There were tears in her eyes and she could hardly see, but through the blur she saw a possible grip just inches from her shoulder. The tiny crystals in the rock seemed huge. She crooked her fingers in the ridge and it held. Then her foot. She rubbed her face on her shoulder and cleared the tears. Another handhold presented itself; so small that only seconds before she would never have risked it, but now she reached. She clung and inched further down.

She knew she had to hurry. Her muscles would not hold out much longer and she had to have somewhere to rest, somewhere that would take her weight. Below her, the red face of the cliff seemed to take on a greenish tinge. She would try to reach the green before she had to stop.

Tekker paid out the rope fraction by fraction. Soon she would have to find a place where she could secure it. He should have brought something with him, a wedge or spike that she could have used to take their weight, but all he had thought of was rope.

'Tekker!'

He jammed the rope with his fist and looked over. She was far out of reach, and almost all he could see of her was her face tilted to look up at him.

'It's moss,' she called, and her voice seemed very tiny. 'The green is moss.'

'Right,' he said. Moss did not seem important.

'You can let down some slack,' she said. 'I can hold you.'

'How?' It was madness talking down into space like this. 'How can you hold me?'

'Loop it over that rock and then come down. I'll take your weight.'

Very carefully, he let the rope go slack against the cliff

face. 'More,' she called. He paid it out until only a short
length remained between his waist and the edge.

'That's all,' he shouted down. 'Now it's me.'

'I've got you.'

As Kit had done, he went over legs first. He left the
rope running as freely as he could around the outcrop, but
did not trust it. He was on his own.

The sound of his breathing came back at him off the
rock and measured his fear. He heard himself panting and
suddenly it sounded like panic. He clung to the vertical
rock, closed his eyes and fought it. He spoke to himself.
One hand, one foot at a time; keep your body close to the
rock.

When his breathing steadied he opened his eyes.

The rock was warm, and the heat of the sun was like
a hand pressing at his back. His confidence began
to creep back and he moved with a rhythm, shifting
his weight from side to side as he came down towards
her.

He paused. She was just below and to one side.

'A bit further,' she said. Her voice seemed to have lost
some of its fear. 'I've still got you.'

Below him the cliff changed from red to green where
the moss made an uneven line. She eased the rope and he
slid one foot down to touch the green. It was thick and
dry. He put his weight on it and it held. He eased down
and reached lower with his other foot.

'Kick,' she said. 'Kick hard.'

He obeyed and felt his toe sink deep. The moss was
tough and closed over his foot to the instep.

'Now you're safe,' she said.

'Safe?' He looked beyond her to the sheer wall that
plunged out of sight. They were insects, so small that for a
moment he thought it would not matter if they fell for the
air would bear them up, then the pain in his fingers made

him realize his weight and the plunge that yawned below. 'We're not safe!'

'Come down.'

He moved lower and grasped the moss. The soft green grew on woody stems. He tugged, but could not tear it free.

'See?' she said. 'As long as you kick hard you're all right.'

He was level with her, his toes wedged securely and both hands with a firm grip. He let some of the tension go, and rested, grinning at her stupidly.

'Still a long way to go,' he said. 'It looks like about a mile.'

Through the streaks of mist that lay like cloud below, they could see the valley floor. It was criss-crossed with gulleys and runnels.

'Are you ready?' she asked, and when he nodded she reached up and flicked the rope so that it snaked free of the outcrop and fell. They wrapped it around their waists so that there was only a short length between them and then they began the descent, kicking and grasping, slowly descending into an unknown land.

16

·

The Palace

Kit, working her way down the sheer face, was having difficulty. Something seemed to be pressing her into the wall. She stopped to consider it.

A yard away to her right Tekker also paused. 'Need a rest?' he asked.

'No.' That was what was odd. She almost felt she could let go and simply lie against the wall without falling off. She twisted to look out across the plain, and then saw what it was. She released one hand, leaned out from the cliff, and waved at him.

'Don't do that!'

His alarm made her laugh. 'We're down,' she said. 'Take a look.'

Cautiously, he eased one elbow from the cliff and turned his head. The wall was no longer quite vertical. It had begun a long curve outwards to meet the valley floor that was still far below. Kit was already shrugging off the rope, leaving him to coil all of it around his own waist, and she started down ahead of him.

'Wait for me!' he called, but she paid no heed. He tried to catch up with her and soon they were racing, slithering as the slope gradually became less steep, and then turning to run on the almost endless ramp of green. The moss became thicker and eventually, breathless, they rolled into a soft cushion that was almost level. They knelt and looked up.

The enormous lift of the cliff made their laughter dwindle and die. It was green and ribbed, like an ocean tilted up against the sky, and the thin ripple of red at its edge was the distant coastline of a foreign country.

'We came from up there.' Kit's voice was very small. 'That's where we live.'

'Except we slid out of it,' he said. The vertical wall stretched from horizon to horizon. 'It's a landslip. It's like being at the bottom of the sea.'

Abruptly, she turned her back on it. 'We've got a long way to go,' she said.

Dan. He saw the thought cloud her eyes as she looked out across the plain. They had still not reached the floor of the valley and a thin, broken haze lay almost level with where they stood. Far away lay the hill of glimmering fragments. But now the setting sun let them see what it was. There were shapes in the glitter. At first they could not make them out and then, gradually, they pieced together shining walls and roofs, pinnacles and bridges, some glaring at them with the full force of the sun, and others letting light flood through them so that they were no more than a shimmer in the air, or the surfaces took the light and changed it into greens and blues or burning, smoky reds.

'It's a city!' said Kit. 'It's on fire!'

'No,' said Tekker. No smoke rose from the blaze. 'It's shining!'

It danced in their eyes, and sometimes they seemed to see right through it.

'Look!'

But Kit's cry was not needed. From the centre of the glittering hill they had gradually become aware that something rose even higher. It was no more than a shimmer rising into the air and standing against the sky, like a great column trying to show itself and not quite succeeding. But now the sun, sinking a fraction nearer the cliffs, caught it, and it was shot through with light. It pulsed with vertical shafts of amber sunshine that blazed to whiteness and robbed their eyes of sight. It was the cause of the soundless explosion.

They shielded their faces, and when they were able to look again it was no more than an image of itself dissolving against the blue.

'What is it?' Kit had both hands shading her eyes. 'There's only bits of it hanging in the air.'

'Platforms,' he said. 'One above the other.' He had once seen parachutists coming down in a spiral as though on a staircase in the sky. It was like that. The transparent platforms were mounted giddily one above the other, but the structure that held them was invisible until the light caught it at an angle to make it flare.

As they looked, even the platforms quivered and vanished, and Kit turned to see Tekker stowing the rope into the haversack.

'We might need it,' he said.

'No.' She shook her head. 'We can't climb something that isn't there.'

'It might be when we reach it.'

'No.' She refused to believe it. 'Not that.' He sat cross-legged on the moss with the haversack in his lap. He was smiling. 'Don't do that,' she said. 'You look mad.'

'Put it this way,' he said. 'If I wasn't laughing I might be crying. Which do you want?'

She stared at him.

'That sounds more like Dan than me,' he said. 'That's how he'd look at it.'

She nodded.

'It was a Dannism,' he said. 'That brother of yours has his uses.' Anything, he thought, to take my mind off where we are. The green plain was gloomy and oppressed him.

Without having to decide what they were going to do, they began to move away from the cliff, striding easily on the tufted moss.

After a while she said, without looking at him, 'Is it true you said that about my nose to Dan? I mean about it not sticking out very much.'

'Funny place to mention it,' he said.

'I don't care. You've been saying things about me, and I want to know.'

'All right, I did say it.'

He fell silent, tormenting her. And when she saw him glance sideways at her, she burst out, 'Well? What about my nose?'

'It's as flat as a cat's.'

'Ugly.'

'I like it,' he said. 'In fact . . .' and he fell silent again.

'In fact what?'

'In fact the other thing's true as well. I told him you were pretty.' She saw him redden, but just as suddenly grin. 'I mean, pretty for Dan's sister.'

'I really hate you, Tekker Begdale.' She began to run.

He chased her. The moss thickened, and soon they were leaping from one springy tuft to another. Suddenly, with a cry, she stumbled and fell headlong between two spongy humps. When she sat up, the surface was above her head. He tried to help her up, but the moss shook under his feet and he managed to balance only by holding on to her.

'It's like being on a treetop,' he said. 'Too unsteady. I'm coming down.'

The woody stems were rooted in ground that was as brown and dry as peat, and the huge tussocks were separated by cracks that meandered everywhere like dried-out streams. They would have to push their way through.

Tekker led. The silence was intense. Even the giant

moss, waist deep, seemed to make no sound as it brushed against them, and there were no insects and no birds. It was a drear place of deep green, and as they waded into it the ground became softer and damp.

'Sun's getting very low,' said Tekker.

For the first time the possibility of being caught in darkness out on the plain crossed their minds. They stopped to take bearings. Far away to their right the cliff was already a black line of shadow. Behind them and to their left it still caught the sun and made a thin red line, but the mists were descending over the plain, and ahead of them the glittering walls had been dimmed to a glimmering mound, like a hump of silver water bubbling out of the ground.

'We shall never see it when it gets dark.' There was alarm in Kit's voice. 'We'll get lost.'

'Wish I'd thought of a compass,' he said.

'Never mind about that now. Let's try and get there.' She tried not to shiver. 'I couldn't stand being out here and not able to see anything.'

They pressed on, and the moss became deeper until it was shoulder height, but they were able to quicken their pace as the gaps between the tussocks broadened. At times they were able to walk side by side, but the further they went the taller the moss became until first Kit and then Tekker could not see above it and they were wandering in a dim, close forest. The ground, that had been no more than spongy, began to ooze moisture, and when Tekker felt it leaking into his shoes he stopped.

'I think there's going to be water ahead,' he said. 'We might as well be ready for it.' They leant against the springy wood of the stems, took off their shoes and socks and he put them in his haversack.

Kit straightened from rolling up the legs of her jeans. Above their heads the sky hardly showed, and down here they were in a dark maze.

'Tekker.' She could not help holding out her hand because she was afraid. He held it. 'How did we come to be in this place?'

'It was me, Kit. I started it.' The dark throats of the tunnels gaped at them. 'I wish I hadn't.'

'So do I.'

They stood still, and the dim tracks meshed them in gloom. Despair seeped into them, and they stood with their shoulders touching and their hands clenched tightly together, holding themselves rigid for fear of what might whisper towards them from the black tunnels.

'We can get out.' Tekker's voice was no more than a croak. 'We can turn the disc.'

'Yes.'

Breathlessly they each waited for the other to make a move. Each yearned to do it. A single nod from either would be enough, and then they would be safe. And share the shame.

Tekker let out his breath in a long sigh, and some of the tension drained from their muscles.

'Dan,' he said. 'I wish he was somebody else's brother.'

'I don't like you, Tekker Begdale. Never did.'

They loosened their hands, glancing slyly at each other, trying to tell if they meant what they said. Then they looked quickly away.

'Onward, then.' He heaved the haversack between his shoulders. 'But which way?'

'There.' Through the dark mesh of stems a faint lightness showed. 'That must come from the palace.'

'Palace?' he said. 'Why do you call it that?'

She shrugged. 'I don't know. Because that's what it is, I suppose.'

They began to walk and the brown peat water oozed between their toes. 'We really are in the fens now,' he said. 'And whoever heard of a palace out in the fens?'

She did not answer. Ahead of them the light was

tantalizing, almost too faint to follow, and she knew they
had to hurry. Very soon, even by jumping, they could not
see above the green roof, and the ground got wetter until
they were splashing ankle-deep in water.

Once they stopped to look back. There was nothing but
darkness closing in behind them, but ahead of them, if
anything, the light was growing brighter. The water
deepened, half way to their knees, and they sent out
waves that rippled and died in the dim tunnels.

It was Tekker who first noticed what was happening.
He shook some of the woody stems. 'This stuff's giving
out,' he said. 'There's reeds ahead.'

The edge of the moss was still distant, but they could
see where it ended in a reed curtain. They pushed on, the
water surging above their knees, and their toes feeling the
beginning of the reed bed.

The sudden brightening of the light as the canopy thinned above them made them slow down. Cautiously they
pushed into the reeds that thickened where they found the
sunlight and grew taller until they reached high
overhead.

Kit looked up. 'Bullrushes,' she said. 'Huge.' The
heavy heads swayed against the sky.

'They'll give us away,' he said. 'Try not to make them
move.'

They went forward along channels where the reeds
grew thinnest, easing themselves between the stems. The
amber sun reached through and put tiger stripes on their
faces and arms as they pushed nearer to the gleam that
drew them. One final curtain remained. They put their
fingers through the green screen and, half crouching,
parted it.

Their vision was obscured. What they saw was upside
down. A palace in water. Bright columns had capsized to
point downwards into a sky so far below it was a bottom-
less blue emptiness that made them cling giddily to the

rushes. Then, barely breathing, they widened the gap and looked across the surface.

A hundred paces away, a ledge of white stone rose just clear of the unrippled water, and from this thin raft the palace sprang. A wall of sheer glass rose straight upwards – a sheet so pure it was like clear water falling from the roof of the sky, but hanging motionless like time stopped, burning with a burst of sun at its base but glistening so high overhead it could have been stars. It had a knife-edge. It seemed too tall to stand. It seemed to sing with the sheer effort of standing in the sky.

Their heads were back. The edge seemed to slice down the sky. They reeled and had to grab the reeds, but the wall had not budged. It stood firm, and now they saw other walls stretching away on either side. All glass, all shot through with colours staining the air, and through the walls they saw columns and hanging balconies, glass buttresses engineered in crimson, amber bridges hanging over crystal space, blue walkways with silvery steps, arches and pinnacles in deep reds that thinned out and dissolved, greens that hung and vanished, and violet that glinted to hard white, then flashed and blinded.

They gazed and never knew how long they stood there. But then, along the base of the nearest wall, just above the white stone platform, they saw the reflection of the reeds and remembered themselves. They pushed through and watched the ripples spread on the clear water. They looked at each other and opened their mouths but did not speak. It took all their breathing to absorb what they saw.

They waded out side by side. The water was above their knees, but the ground under their feet had become smooth and level. The ripples spread out, fading into the long lake that stretched away on either side, but the water did not deepen and soon the ripples washed at the stone platform's edge.

They hesitated to touch it, as though the huge

dynamo of the palace, pulsing with light as the setting sun flared on new angles, had charged the stone with its power, but when they reached out it was warm only with the heat of the long day. It was chest height. Tekker put both hands on it, heaved himself from the water, and reached down to help Kit.

They stood on the warm stone. Fifty paces separated them from the glass wall which, they now saw, had buttresses of solid glass more than twice the span of their arms in thickness but so pure they were almost invisible. A cascade of glass hung above them.

'I see us.' Kit's voice was the only sound. She pointed.

At the foot of the wall there was a ridge of darkness. She lifted her hand above her head and something moved there. Tekker was startled until he saw what it was. Their own shapes were reflected back at them, standing against the background of dark bullrushes.

They went forward, seeing themselves mirrored, their jeans rolled to their knees and wet. Tekker looked down and saw the footprints they were leaving. It was real.

'But there's no way inside,' he said. 'We can't get in.'

They were at the edge of one of the buttresses. It was bedded deep in the stone, but not into darkness. As hard as stone itself, but as clear as air, it let light down into the square pit where it rested its weight. They touched it. It was like touching still water, invisible except to their fingertips. They smoothed it with their hands and lifted their eyes to look along its surface.

They saw the amber haze over the plain reflected in it like a picture, and further away the horizon and the deepening blue of the sky. And then, together, they froze.

Dark shapes were moving there, coming at their backs with long, slow wingbeats.

17
·
The Visitor

They had to get out. Tekker wasted no time turning to face the danger. Twisting would jam the disc and purse even tighter in his jeans pocket and he kept his eyes riveted on the reflection as he dug for it.

Kit saw what he was doing and stepped back and turned as though she could give him extra seconds by putting herself between him and what was speeding towards them. The Horseheads in their machines came low, skimming the plain and leaving the mist in a spiralling trail behind them.

She saw him fumble with the purse. 'Be quick!' she cried. They had no chance of hiding. There was the glass wall behind them, and in front was the wide expanse of white stone and placid water.

'Quick!' From the corner of her eye she saw him pulling at the drawstring of the purse. A lifting and dipping black army swept closer. She heard the whistle of the wingtips and the creak and groan of the mechanisms.

The first of them lifted to clear the tall rushes. Tekker saw its wings in the glass, then another and another tilt up into the sky. He had the purse open. His fingers closed on the disc.

'Tekker!'

It was a scream. The first was on them. The wings were wide, checking its flight. The head was tilted down,

seeking them out. She went backwards, pushing against
him as the disc turned in his fingers. He put a hand
against the smooth wall to stop himself falling, unable to
turn, and saw it all happen in the glass.

The wings beat upward, ragged in the reflection, and
others came, flying alongside until there was a circling
mass above them. He pushed back as the first harsh cries
came from the sky.

There were houses. Across the flat stone there were
houses. The stone platform was a roadway.

Kit stood on the pavement. He himself was in a shop
doorway and its window reflected the sky. Rooks beat
overhead, opening their bills to cry hoarsely in the sky as
they circled above tall trees.

Across the road, an old man sat on a kitchen chair
outside the front door of his cottage. He had his legs
crossed and his arms folded, and he was watching them.

'Where are we?' Kit spoke to Tekker, but her voice was
louder than she intended and the old man answered her.

'That's a rum 'un if you don't know that much.' He had
a grey moustache and a bristled chin, which he rubbed
with one thick finger. 'Where you from?'

Kit glanced up at the rooks and then pointed down the
road away from the church. 'Just from there,' she said.

'I been sat in the sun for a half-hour, and I never see
you come.'

'Must have had your eyes closed,' said Tekker. 'Perhaps you dropped off for a minute.'

The man ignored that. 'Rum pair, you are,' he said.
'Look as though you've been down a dyke to me.'

'Makes a change,' said Tekker. 'Got tired of sticking to
the roads all the way to Manea.'

'At least one of you knows what place you're at. I was
beginning to wonder if you wasn't a pair of loonies got free
from somewhere.'

'Well I reckon we are.' Tekker had seen a spark of amusement in the old man's eye, and his confidence grew. 'We were looking for a palace.' He heard Kit draw in her breath and he made a face at her. Something had connected in his mind.

'Palace?' said the man. 'What palace?'

'Well, not exactly a palace. It was never built.'

'Oh *that* palace,' said the old man. 'Why didn't you say?'

'Well I don't suppose you ever saw it, as it wasn't there.'

'No. Never did.'

They were going to go on like this. Kit could see it. 'Please!' she said. 'What's all this about?'

Tekker had a glint in his eye to match the old man's, but he became serious. 'There was going to be a palace out here at Manea,' he said. 'Once they'd drained the fens.'

Kit knew. 'But that was four hundred years ago,' she said. 'King Charles.'

'Oh him,' said the man.

'Know him?' said Tekker.

'I know him. Him and all them titled lot. They reckoned they was going to have a right old time once they drained them marshes. Build a palace! Load of old squit.' He spat into the dust by his chair.

'Never came to anything,' said Tekker.

'Lords and rich men,' said the man. 'Think they can do what they want. Load of old squit. All on 'em.'

'Fenmen didn't like it.'

'Took away their living,' said the man. 'Fought like tigers, they did, and there never was a palace.'

'It never got to be more than an idea in somebody's mind,' said Tekker.

'Damn good job, an' all,' said the man. 'Squit.'

Kit was tugging at Tekker, and as they moved away he
said to the man, 'Got to get home,' but the man ignored
him.

'He's a fen tiger,' said Tekker. 'They never liked lords.'

'You shouldn't tell people so much.' They had pulled
on their shoes and were running, leaving the village
behind. 'They'll think we're mad.'

'It's true about the palace. The king was going to call it
Charlemont.'

'They cut off his head,' she said. 'Good job.'

'All fen tigers agree with that.' He was panting as they
ran to where the signal box made a landmark among flat
fields. 'But it was an idea. And ideas grow. Perhaps that's
what started off John Welbeck and his Stella.'

'I don't care.' Kit was the force that was driving them.
'We've got to get home and get ready for tonight.'

'Tonight?' His mind was on palaces.

'We can't do anything until it gets dark. Those
Horseheads would see us.'

There were wisps of evening mist over the dykes as they
went back across the flat land, keeping to the road and
jogging until they met the gentle slope up to the level
crossing. It slowed them, and for a few paces they
staggered until they saw the man in the signal box
watching them with curiosity. They straightened and
walked across the line, talking to each other as though
there was nothing unusual in strolling so far out here.

They found their bikes in the dyke, and as they rode
away their long shadows pointed the way to the village.
Under cover of darkness they would come this way again.

There was a scattering of people on the bridge and
along the railings. They hesitated, not wanting to speak
to anybody, but there was no avoiding it.

'Where've you two been, then?' somebody asked.

'Just out,' said Tekker. 'Out and about.'

'I'll bet.' Betty Sutton stood close to Wilf Piggins. 'You

been doing more than just ride them bicycles.'

'Looking for ghosts, I reckon,' said a voice from the waterside.

'Yeah,' said Betty.

'And that reminds me.' Wilf pushed himself clear of the railings. 'I seen somebody this afternoon who was interested in you, Begdale.' With Betty beside him, he had brought the malice back into his voice. 'Very interested.'

'Who's that?'

Wilf ignored him and spoke to Kit: 'Your brother ain't very well, is he?'

She murmured something but Tekker broke across her. 'Who wanted to know about me?'

'Well now.' Wilf rested one elbow against the parapet. 'That would be telling.'

'Then tell.' Tekker slid off the saddle and stood beside his bicycle.

'You're going to enjoy this, Begdale.' Wilf took his time. 'I met old Ma Grist along the road, so I asked her about stray horses, didn't I?'

He paused, and skinny Lenny came out of his shadow to praise him. 'That took a bit of nerve, Wilf.'

'Well,' Wilf made light of it, 'I wanted to know, didn't I? But she come at me like a hellcat. Right up to me face. Got a claw into me shoulder so as I could hardly move. When? she said. Where? Why? I never seen anything like the way she went on.'

'And you told her.' Tekker had lowered his bike to the ground.

'Why not? I ain't got nothing to hide.'

'Oh yes you have, Piggins. You got a big yellow stripe right down your back.'

Tekker stepped forward, but behind him another bike fell and suddenly Kit was in front of him.

'No!' she said. 'Not now! You've got to think of Dan!'

As Kit came between them, Wilf had pushed himself

upright, but when Tekker eased himself free of her grasp, Wilf once again subsided to lean against the parapet.

Tekker stood with Kit alongside him. 'Well, Wilf?' he said.

'Not with your mate ill, Begdale. Not if he's that bad.' His eyes did not meet Tekker's.

'That's right, Wilf.' Lenny propped up his hero. 'Let him go. It wouldn't be right. Dan's pretty ill, ain't he?'

Tekker turned his back on them. There was a hush as he and Kit picked up their bikes, and as they rode away they heard Wilf's voice raised behind them in a last effort to hold his place with the others. 'I had to let him go, didn't I? He ain't worth a light. Let the old woman deal with him.'

Tekker looked sideways at Kit. 'The old woman's not going to get a chance,' he said, but Kit's face was pale and set and she did not reply.

The gravel of the driveway crunched under their tyres as they turned in at her gateway and they looked up at Dan's window. The curtains were closed, and whatever light there was inside burned too dimly to show. The frosted glass panels of the kitchen door showed someone sitting at the table, and Kit caught her breath, afraid of what she might be told as she entered.

'How is he now, Mum?' But the words faltered and she was jarred to a standstill. It was not her mother.

The round face with thin-rimmed glasses smiled at her. 'We've been wondering where you were, dear,' said Ma Grist.

Neither of them spoke.

'You're a bit late home, dear.' The little features in the broad face flickered again into a smile. 'Your mother's worried about you.'

'What are you doing here?' It was almost a shout. Kit stepped into the kitchen. 'Where's my mother?'

'Hush, child!' It was a bitter little whisper, but again

her features writhed into something that pretended to be friendly. 'Your mother's upstairs with your poor brother. I just stepped in to ask after him.'

'No you didn't! You wanted to make sure he was worse!'

Kit was on the point of lunging, but Tekker held her arm.

'There now, dear.' The voice was soothing and the lips were curved upwards, but bright anger shone in her eyes. 'The young man knows how to behave. No need to fly at me just because you're upset, my little dove. What will be, will be.'

'I hate you!'

'It will do no good, my darling. You should be hating whoever it was caused him to be like this in the first place.'

'You!'

'No, no, no.' She had taken off her brown hat, and as she shook her head she gazed down at it in her lap. 'Whoever could have told you such stuff and nonsense about me, my dear?' She raised her head and for the first time her eyes rested full on Tekker.

'Somebody said you were looking for me,' he said.

'Was I? Was I really?' Her attention suddenly switched off. Her small mouth, button nose and eyes were no more than fingermarks pressed into the flesh of her face.

'He told you about what we saw.'

'And what was that?' The eyes remained closed.

Tekker's throat had tightened, and his voice was feeble. 'The stray horse,' he said.

Behind the glass of her spectacles, as though some slow creature had shifted under water to allow bright pebbles to show, her eyes gradually opened. 'Yes,' she said. 'You came snooping. You and your friend.' She waited until Tekker nodded. 'You saw something, and you thought it was . . .' She left the sentence for him to finish.

'A stray horse,' he said.

'Of course it was.' Her smile was suddenly fierce and directed at Kit. 'I was kind to the poor creature, my love. I did not wish it harm – nor harm to anything.'

Kit's mouth opened, but Tekker jerked at her arm to silence her, and the voice went on.

'Just a stray horse. But they had to come snooping.'

There was a movement upstairs.

'Oh, the poor boy,' she said and sat solidly in her tight brown coat, gazing straight ahead. 'I hope nobody else gets the same affliction.' She sighed and raised the hat and a long steel hatpin from her lap, murmuring and shaking her head. 'And there's that poor man who lives up the road.'

'John Welbeck?' said Tekker.

She nodded. 'He's not too well. Not too well at all.' Absently, she ran the long hatpin into the felt of her hat. 'They tell me he went somewhere where he had no business to go and something happened to him.' The pin glinted as she pulled it out and bent her head forward to put on her hat. 'And now nobody but me can go near him. He won't let them. It's a very great shame.' The gleaming pin vanished through hat and hair, and she straightened. 'People should never go where they don't belong. Never.'

She got to her feet, and slowly came towards them. They fell back to allow her to pass, but she stopped in front of them. Tekker saw a vein pulsing in the smooth, plump skin of her neck, and the little mouth had stretched to put a pale dimple in each cheek. 'I hear your mother coming, my dear. I don't think I need bother her any longer. I must just pop in on poor Mr Welbeck.'

She was moving past when Kit cried, 'Dan! What's going to happen to Dan?'

She turned at the door. 'What will be, will be,' she said.

18

·

Under the Dome

At home, Tekker had to take a chance. He faced an avalanche of questions about Dan from his mother, and he fended them off by telling her he was going to bed early because he wanted to be with Dan first thing in the morning.

'He must be bad, then?' she said.

'Bad enough.'

She clucked her tongue, but she ceased to pay much attention because she was getting ready to go out with his father, changing her dress, putting on make-up and leaving a wake of perfume wherever she went.

'You smell nice,' he said, aiming to keep her in a good mood.

'I'll tuck you in, my pet,' she patted his cheek as she whisked past, 'when we come home.'

'You'd better not.' He glowered at her. 'I don't want you waking me up in the middle of the night.'

'There's a surly face for me to leave behind.' She was teasing him. 'Very well.' She pecked his cheek. 'That'll have to do.'

'Promise?'

'Promise.' And she and his father were gone.

The dusk was already deepening and he did not have much time. He had already taken the large torch that his father kept in the car, and he put it in his haversack with a sandwich box crammed with bread and butter and cake. Kit was bringing apples. He took his clasp knife. It would not be much of a weapon but it would have to do. He found a piece of cord in his father's desk and, in a trick that his father had taught him from his Navy days, he made a lanyard for it so he could wear it around his waist. That way he would not lose it, and it would be ready to hand.

Then he took some cushions from the settee and went up to his bedroom. They made a fairly convincing shape in his bed, but to make it safer he wrote a 'Do not disturb' notice in large letters and pinned it to his door.

None of the neighbours saw him leave and soon he was cycling along the back lanes to the place where he would meet Kit. He had almost left the village when the sight of a telephone box made him stop. There was one thing that had not occurred to either of them.

He propped his bike alongside the kiosk and found John Welbeck's number. He dialled it. It rang for so long he could almost hear it echoing in a house where the old man was either too ill to answer it, or worse. Then suddenly the receiver was lifted and the pips began. He pressed the coin into the slot and opened his mouth to speak but, before any sound came, a voice which was not John Welbeck's said, 'Who's that?'

Ma Grist. Tekker put a hand over the mouthpiece. She must not even hear him breathing.

'Hello.'

He did not answer.

'Who's there?'

No answer.

There was a pause in which he felt his hand go clammy. Then there was a grunt, the phone rattled in its cradle, and silence. Even the warm evening chilled his skin as he stepped outside.

There was a gate in a hedge where they had promised to meet. He was early, but Kit was already there.

'We can't get to Mr Welbeck,' he said. 'She's in his house with him.'

Kit did not seem to hear. 'Dan's worse,' she said. Her face was very pale and she held herself stiffly. 'They wanted me out of the way so I pretended to go to bed early. They're both with him.' Her voice was getting quieter as she spoke until she was almost whispering. 'I think they might have to get an ambulance.'

He saw that she wanted to run home, crying. His stomach shrank and he fought to stop himself trembling. 'So they won't miss you.' He heard his own voice. It sounded heartless. 'What did you bring?'

She turned away to her bicycle and handed him apples from the basket on the handlebars. There was a pullover underneath, and as she gave it to him to stow away with his, she said, 'I tried to get my father's shotgun, but it's locked up.'

'I've got my knife.'

Their eyes met. Knives and guns. It had come to that. He saw her face harden as she accepted it. Nothing would stop her fighting for Dan.

'Are we going to stand here all night?' she said. 'Or are we going to try to get there while we can still see something?'

He told her again about the phone call as they rode, and the threat to John Welbeck sent them speeding faster into the twilight.

Not all the light had gone from the sky, and the lonely signal box guarded a silvery line that dwindled to darkness. The plain was gathering a thin night-covering of shadows and, as they approached the village, only the tops of the trees stood plainly on the horizon. At the roadside, the old man had long ago taken his

kitchen chair inside, and the door of his cottage was shut.
They went past the shop and left their bicycles by the church wall. The rooks had ceased to circle and no traffic stirred as they returned to stand near the shop window.

Tekker still had the purse. He handed it to Kit.

'Now?' she asked.

He nodded, and as she drew its strings and took out the disc, he watched the cottage across the road. Suddenly it seemed to retreat, sliding backwards across a smooth surface until its windows shrank and dimmed, then narrowed and stretched until they were as thin as reeds. Then it was gone, and the shadows of bullrushes mingled with the stars reflected in the still water.

Kit was looking upwards. The glass wall seemed no longer solid. It was like a shimmering curtain hung across the sky, more grey than blue, and trembling with stars.

'I saw it all happen,' he said. 'Everything seemed to fold and turn over. Just like pages in a book.'

She had taken the pouch and was putting it in her pocket. 'I can't see any patrols,' she said.

He was half way between one world and another, but the danger of the black wings made him cease trying to see the cottage among the rushes.

He turned and stepped closer to the huge wall. It was almost invisible. The last of the sun, sloping into the palace, showed them what was beyond it but they found themselves putting their hands out to touch it and make sure that it rose in front of them. It was many feet thick, yet through it they could see a floor of a different colour to the stone they stood on, a liquid blue, and in the distance the broken light of many shafts and columns.

'Which way?' Tekker asked. 'Left or right?'

Kit pointed. 'I think I see a mark on the stone.'

He saw it, too. A dark line stretched from the still water of the moat towards the wall and seemed to vanish inside.

'Could be a shadow,' he said. 'Might be a path. Anyway we've got no choice.' They advanced to the foot of the wall. 'You know what I feel like?' he said. 'A beetle on a window ledge. I can almost hear our tiny feet scraping.'

'*Your* tiny feet. I'm silent.'

'You want me to shut up?'

'You're talking a lot.'

He breathed deeply and looked up at another towering buttress that went up in a series of steps like a frozen cascade. 'I always talk when I'm enjoying myself. I can't help it. And this is marvellous.' He walked on a few steps. 'All we need is Dan.'

Kit's attention was on the line of the shadow, chasing thoughts of Dan out of her head. 'I see what it is,' she said. 'It's a river.'

'More like a canal.' He saw a channel cut into the stone with a broad path on either side. 'It's got to go somewhere.'

The angle of the huge buttress distorted their view and they moved out to see round it. Another buttress lay beyond, but between them, like two straining giants, they supported a towering arch.

'That's it!' he said. 'The way in!'

But they hung back. It was too huge. They would drift inside like two grains of dust, and be lost. Then the sun, going down behind the cliffs far away, caught the high arch and made it burn red and poured gold down through the buttress to spill out over the stone towards them. It seemed like a welcome, and Kit led the way. The warmth drew her, but she also realized that they could hide in the dazzle, for no enemy would gaze for long into the brightest places.

'Quick, Tekker, while it lasts!'

They ran into the glare. It was like a furnace. Flames of

sunlight licked and flared through the walls, blazed in the water and reddened the broad stone path until they seemed to run on ash. Deeper and deeper they plunged into the glare and suddenly, still dazzled, they were through.

Space opened up, and coolness touched their skin. They were on the other side of the wall and under the sky. Then they looked up. There was a milky whiteness above that was not the sky. Shadowy ribs curved high overhead, reaching as far as they could see and holding a membrane of white glass. They were under a dome in a vast hall.

'It's dark,' Kit whispered. 'I'm cold.'

They stood close together and the glare of the tall entrance at their backs threw long shadows over the circular floor but faded into dimness before it touched the far side. All they saw was space and a curved wall, mottled with shadows, rising to the pale whiteness.

At their feet the floor was patterned in black and white stone, but a few paces from them it shone as though it had been polished. Then Tekker realized why.

'It's water!' he said. 'This whole hall is a pond.' The channel from the moat outside joined a circular lake under the dome.

Kit shuddered. 'I don't like it,' she said, but Tekker had already begun to move forward. 'Come back!'

Her cry echoed and died away into the distance, and brought him to a standstill near the water's edge.

'It seems to be quite shallow,' he whispered. 'We could wade across it, if we have to.'

'No!' Water and darkness were a nightmare. 'We'll keep to the wall.' Now that her eyes were growing used to the dimness she saw that a row of massive columns stood just clear of the wall and rose to join the ribs of the dome. There was space between the columns and the wall for them to walk clear of the water.

But Tekker was leaning forward, straining to see into the dark cave of the hall. 'There's something in the middle.'

'What? I can't see.' She had moved out alongside him and her fingers feverishly clutched his arm.

'I don't know. But at least it's not moving.' He crouched to look along the surface of the water. 'Trees, I think.'

She crouched with him. He was right. There were trees out there, dotted about in the water, but made to look tiny by the size of the dome.

'And something else,' he said. 'Like a huge plant. Two of them.' She looked along his arm and saw flat shapes resting on the water. They were pale and round. 'Like white leaves,' he said. 'Lily pads.'

'They're too big.' She was drawing him back. 'Lilies have never been that size.'

'But they might be in here, Kit.'

'We're not going to find out.' She tugged him with her into the colonnade, and they began to move along it.

They walked almost silently in caves of darkness formed by the huge columns, but even the tiny sounds they made whispered back at them and from time to time they stopped and listened.

'Nobody here but us,' he breathed, but once again he crouched to look out across the floor of still water. 'There's more of them, Kit. More lily pads.'

She could see them, ghostly and silvery, riding on the surface, and so faint they seemed constantly on the verge of moving. 'I want to get out of here.' She pressed on, and soon they were hurrying, on the verge of trotting.

The columns went by like a funeral procession, and the pattering of their feet was the sound of mice in an empty church. Kit could feel panic in her throat and when Tekker suddenly pulled up and held her back she struggled to run on.

'We're almost there, Kit.'

'Where?' She had lost all idea of direction.

'The way out. I can see it.'

The columns stood on square plinths, taller than they were, and they edged along the side of one and looked out. Across the curve of the water's edge, set back between two columns, a tall oblong of darkness gaped.

'There's another canal,' he said. 'That's where it goes.'

She could see where the rim of the lake was interrupted, and the channel disappeared through the portal.

'But it's jet black.' She held him back.

'Not much worse than out here.' The dome still showed dark ribs against milky whiteness high above, but the floor below had silted up with darkness. Even the bright entrance had long since vanished.

'We're going to need the torch whichever way we go.' He unslung the haversack as he spoke, and he took out the torch and handed it to her.

They crept closer, stepping silently, and stood in the mouth of the opening. Within two paces, the blackness was raised in front of them like something they could touch, and it hid everything beyond. She turned to face him.

'Should I?' she asked, and when he nodded she shielded the torch with her fingers and sent a thin beam inside. It touched the water of the canal and glinted and glanced away into the darkness, where it died. It reached nothing.

'Try the full beam, Kit. We might not have very far to go.' He kept his voice low, but the high tunnel took it and echoed the last word over and over in its throat until it became a moan and dwindled into silence.

She said nothing, but unshielded the torch and pointed it. The water roadway was glassy and endless, but on either side of it there was a broad path. She switched off and looked back. The light from above barely reached the floor, and the hall was full of shadows. Whatever happened, they could not go back.

'We'd better hold hands,' she whispered, and their fingers interlocked as she switched on the torch.

Side by side they stepped deeper into the tunnel. Their shoes were soft-soled but every footfall, and even the rustle of their clothes, made the still air vibrate like a drumskin and whisper ahead the news that they were coming.

She kept the beam shielded and pointed downwards, but once her fingers slipped and the light threw Tekker's shadow across the black water to the wall on the far side. For a split second it seemed like a walker on the other path and her gasp yawned away into the distance.

He put his head close to hers and whispered, 'I'm too near the water, Kit. The path's getting narrow.'

She flicked the beam upwards. 'And the roof's lower.' It was closing in. She pointed it ahead. 'Tekker, the path gives out! We can't go on!'

Suddenly he reached and covered the lens. 'Switch it off, Kit! Quick!'

Blackness seemed to collapse on them. She felt its pressure. She struggled to turn and start back but he held her.

'What!' The word came out in panic.

'Hush!'

The echo of their voices died. But a new sound came, faintly, in the distance, tiptoeing towards them from behind.

19

·

A Thin Shell

It came again, a swift patter of footsteps.

'Now!'

Kit flicked on the light. The tunnel showed sharply and the footsteps ceased. The paths were smooth. And bare. Nothing moved or crouched.

'Off!'

They waited in darkness, listening. Nothing stirred.

In the silence, Tekker tried to free his knife. He fumbled with the lanyard around his waist but his fingers were thick and clumsy.

The sound came again. A rush of faint footsteps echoing and dying. Then silence.

Kit's finger was on the button, but she waited. Tekker had the knife through the loop but it slid through his fingers, dragging the cord with it, and fell. It clattered on the stone at his feet as the sound came again. A slithering thin chuckle. Closer.

Tekker crouched, sweeping the ground with his hands, but in the blackness he had lost even the wall. His senses were confused. Wherever he reached there seemed to be an edge and water.

Whatever was coming dragged its feet now, scraping towards them, and Kit could hold out no longer. She switched on.

The beam showed the roof and both walls. The paths

were empty. She pointed it at the channel. Something was
sliding towards them on the water. It was on the far side.
Black and squat. The beam touched it and it seemed to
pause, surprised. Then a gleam flickered at its edge, there
was a quick, rattling scrape, and it came for them.

Tekker stood and yelled. Kit screamed. They had no
defence.

Its snout pushed out a ripple. Kit raised the torch,
ready to strike, and its light touched the roof and flooded
down. The shape in the water was pale. It turned slowly
and touched the edge. The quick rasp and rattle reached
them as it moved into the channel again, still turning.

It was then Kit saw what it was.

'From the lake!' Her voice was hoarse. 'We saw it! A
leaf!'

But huge, and silvery now. She shone the torch full on
it. It was not quite circular; not a lily pad, and it was
hard. Its brittle rim tapped like footsteps along the stone
edge of the canal.

Suddenly Tekker was full length on the stone. 'Where's
my knife?' he shouted. 'I can't see it!'

Quickly she shone the torch on the ground. The knife
and its lanyard lay by his side, and she put them in his
hand.

'There's a current,' he said. 'It's coming on the current.
I want it.'

He had looped the cord around his wrist and was
swinging the knife just clear of the water. The silvery leaf
drifted down, crossing to touch the far bank, and then
spinning slowly towards them.

It was going by out of reach. He swung the knife. It
landed over the edge of the floating shell and he pulled.
The shape swung and the knife dislodged itself and the
huge leaf drifted by. He scrambled on all fours after it and
swung again. The knife went over its lip and lodged. He

eased his fingers along the cord, pulling it in, and slowl
the edge of the shape came nearer. His fingers touched an
he held tight.

'Help me,' he said. The current, which they had no
noticed until now, was stronger than he had thought.

She lay down beside him and held the floating shape. It
rim stood a hand's span above the water, and even in th
uncertain light of the torch lying on the path alongside he
she could see that a fan of veins spread from a point in it
centre.

'It *is* a leaf,' she said. Some gigantic lily had shed a leaf a
hard and transparent as glass and as thick as her thumb.

'It's a boat,' he said. It was oval and hollow, twice hi
height in length.

'Leaf,' she said.

'Boat.'

At least it was no monster. He started to laugh, and sh
giggled with him until the tunnel bubbled with the sound

'Can you hold it?' he asked.

'Yes.'

He got to his knees and put the lanyard around his waist
threading the knife through the loop. 'It's a leaf *and* a boat,
he said. 'A leaf boat.'

'It'll never hold us.'

'We can try. And anyway I don't think the water's ver
deep.' He took the torch and shone it down. 'I can see th
bottom.'

She wanted to draw back but, unless they waded in th
dark water, the leaf was the only way of going on. She hel
it still, and he got down at the edge of the canal and put on
foot on to the thin shell. Then, holding her arm, he steppe
down. His weight made it dip and rock and she had to hol
on tight, but he released her arm and squatted, holding or
to both upturned edges of the leaf. It had hardly sunk ar
inch deeper.

'It's safe,' he said. 'Like a raft.'

'It's getting hard to hold.'

He stood, leant over, and put both elbows on the stone. 'Now you. Give me the torch.'

He held it so that it shone into the silvery centre. The leaf looked too fragile to take both of them, but she stepped down, clinging to him.

'Sit in the middle,' he said. 'That'll steady it.'

She sat cross-legged and gripped both edges.

'Now me.'

He had warned her, but still she almost cried out as the front of the leaf reared up as he slid down behind her. She shuffled quickly forward and it settled, almost level.

The torch had fallen from his grasp and lay between them shining through the transparent keel into the water beneath. The craft began to turn, but as the wall swung near he fended it off.

'We need an oar,' he said. 'We can't steer.'

They had drifted slowly to the other side and Kit had to reach out to stop them touching.

'Give me the torch,' she said. 'We've got to see where we're going.'

He handed it to her and she shone it ahead. Already the paths had disappeared and the tunnel's walls were closer. Suddenly she had to snatch her hand away from the edge to prevent it being jammed. They were going faster and she had no time to fend it off. The leaf hit the wall a glancing blow and she jerked back, ready for it to shatter. But the thud merely sent a quiver along its length and it sped on.

'Strong,' he said. 'Tougher than it looks.'

'Needs to be.' The words came in a gasp, for the shell had gained speed and was already going too fast for her to risk leaning out. But the shift of her weight had made the leaf veer, and instinctively she leant the other way. The bows came round. She checked the swing and the boat held straight.

Tekker had seen what she did. It was like riding a bicycle, and he straightened his legs along the bottom of the boat on either side of her, put his arms around her waist and swayed with her, following her directions, as she kept the bows pointing into the centre of the blackness.

There was sound now. The water was whispering along the stone, flowing faster as the walls gradually pushed closer. Ripples broke from the sides and streamed towards the middle, and then they became little waves which angled out and held the boat in the centre of the current. And they gained speed. They could feel the air pushing at their faces.

She switched off the torch.

'Why did you do that!' Tekker was alarmed.

'I can see a light!' She had to lean back to make herself heard. The water was breaking up in the narrow tunnel and its roar echoed around them.

He saw the gleam directly ahead, but the roaring darkness filled him with fear. 'I can't see where we're going!' he yelled, and she switched on.

Within a few seconds the water had boiled to white rapids. They could feel it punch the craft, knocking it first one way and then another and at times putting a great fist of water in their path to shock them almost to a standstill. But Kit fought the turmoil, heeling to meet a white ridge, steadying over broken water, slipping into a hollow and riding out of it wet with spray. She was in charge, and he swayed with her as the walls skimmed past and the beam she held tossed and lurched in the tunnel.

A sickening shock and a lash of spray shut his eyes. He felt a tilt and a smooth slide and knew they were sinking. He gulped air and tensed himself to meet the rush of water.

But it did not come, and he opened his eyes as the smooth

slide continued. They were spinning gently under the stars. The last turbulence as they left the tunnel had pushed them almost flat in the bottom of the boat, and Kit elbowed herself upright.

'Listen,' she said.

He could hear the rush of water in the tunnel's mouth, but it was already receding.

'We're still moving,' she said.

'But the water's calm. Quite flat.' He could detect no movement. They seemed to be afloat on an immense lagoon.

'What's that?' Once again, as they circled slowly, Kit was the first to see what lay ahead.

It stood in the sky like the stars itself, but brighter, a stream of light, broad at its base but thinning as it lifted, and dwindling to nothingness. It was a tower made of the hanging platforms they had seen blaze in the sun, but now it had its own light, ghostly and faint.

The boat swung it out of sight, but circled until they faced it again. Its base was a hill of glimmering colours, but it rose beyond the hilltop, lifting to pierce the night like a spear.

They swung again, and Tekker drew in his breath sharply.

'What is it?' She twisted towards him, but he did not answer. He reached forward suddenly and took the torch from her. 'What are you doing?'

The ray from the torch was waving across the sky like a pointer. 'I saw something. It was hanging in the air.' She snatched at his hand and slid his finger on the button. The light went out. 'Why did you do that?'

'Quiet!' She forced the torch down. 'Listen!'

The water lapped against the veins of their thin boat but she steadied it until the rocking ceased. As the silence spread outwards, he heard what had made her plunge them into darkness. A sigh that was no more than a wisp of sound came from far away. It faded and came again, and then again, pulsing in a long beat. And getting louder. It swung behind them and came from the other side. A rushing of air. A pause. A creak. And then the rushing again.

Suddenly she knew what it was, but he had wrenched his hand from hers. The beam flashed on and he was pointing it towards the sound.

'Put it out!' she cried. 'Put it out!'

But still he strove to pierce the darkness. 'Why?'

'Because they see it! They're coming at it!'

The beam, arcing over the water, touched something. It was blackness against blackness, palpitating in the dark. And then something else. A pale dot. He centred on it, holding steady. To either side of the white smudge the darkness rippled as though the night itself was folding towards them in layer upon layer, and as it swept forward, the shape sharpened. A horse's skull rode at them through the creak and sigh of the air.

He lost it. The boat was turning. A whistling rush split the air overhead, and he lifted the beam.

The Horsehead gazed at them. Black eye sockets and ragged snout. It dipped. He flung the torch with all his force. A tilted surface billowed over the water like a black sail. The torch struck its edge. They heard it thud and saw it spin away, end over end, until with a splash that was lost in the rushing darkness, it went out.

The wingbeats lifted and a shape flickered across the stars, wheeling in a wide circle. They were hidden in the darkness, but it would come again.

The boat spun and brought the glittering hill and tower in view. They were closer.

'We're moving!' he shouted. He felt air brushing him. 'Fast!'

'What's that!' Against the glittering pile she saw a silhouette of something jutting from the water. It was a blunt post.

'There's another.' He pointed away to one side. 'There's more.' He saw a double row of posts, a harbour entrance, but the boat would sweep by. 'Steer!' He lunged over the side and thrust his arm deep in the water.

She lifted her eyes to find the shape in the sky. It blotted out the stars, swooping to cut them off from the harbour.

'We can't make it!'

'Steer!'

She lurched with him as the boat reared and came round like a cavorting horse. But the shape was on them, its bulk blocking the way and dipping to scoop them.

'Pull!' he yelled, and together they thrust their arms to the shoulder in the water and hauled back. They skewed sideways but the move was too late. A wing hit them. It scythed along the side of the boat, lifting it high, and water poured in.

They lunged forward to right it as the wing tore free, and in the light from the glowing hillside they clung help-lessly and watched.

The clash had unsteadied the flying machine. It staggered in the air. One wingtip touched the water, strained to free itself, but failed. It bit deep and the wide-spread wings were jarred into a cartwheel. The nose plunged and, with a shuddering jerk, the wings collapsed. Like a black tent caught in a flood, the whole structure was swept towards the pillars. They saw it catch the base of one column and pile itself into jagged fragments, and then the swirl of water swept them by.

20
·
Thunder in Darkness

As they swung into the track marked by the black posts they searched the darkness, but nothing kept pace with them through the air or crossed against the stars.

'The current's faster,' he said. The posts went by like a procession of dark, shrouded figures with water lapping at their feet. 'But I think we're safe.'

'Except we're almost sinking.' She had shuffled to crouch in the water in the bottom of the boat and was baling out with her hands. 'Help me.'

He knelt behind her, but the haversack unbalanced him and the boat rocked dangerously.

'Take it off!' she said.

As he struggled out of the straps and put the haversack down between them she held the edges of the frail shell. Her fingers touched the surface of the water outside.

'That haversack's too much weight,' she said. 'Get rid of it.'

'It's all our supplies. Everything.'

'I don't care!'

'I thought we were coming into a harbour.' He looked ahead but the mountain was still distant. He tried to calculate how far, but even as he did so the craft rocked and more water lapped over the edge.

'Throw it out!'

He balanced himself carefully and lowered the haversack overboard. It floated alongside them for a moment, and then a swirl clutched it and twisted it away into the darkness like a drowned man. He clenched his teeth, trying not to shudder, and was leaning forward to begin baling when he paused. He could hear water gurgling as it pushed at the posts. It was moving faster. And something else.

'Kit.' She stopped baling and raised her head. 'We're tilting.' She clung tight, ready to shift her weight, but he said, 'Not us. The water.'

The surface, ribbed by the posts, told her nothing, but when she looked ahead she saw it. They were sliding downhill. The whole lagoon had tilted and was slipping with them. Her head jerked from side to side seeking a way they could dig at the water and pull themselves free, but it was too late. Grumbling thunder reached them from ahead. The lagoon plunged into a chasm.

Tekker clutched her round the waist. 'Keep still!' he shouted. 'Lean back!'

They had no choice. The leaf boat had slanted forward and they slid on the tilted water as it spun itself into thick ropes that whipped and jolted them towards the yawning blackness. They were helpless. The boat slid faster as the water fell away steeper and steeper until they barely seemed to be touching it and then they were flung free, soaring in air over the final drop.

Tekker felt Kit's nails dig into his arms as he tightened his grip around her waist. But clinging was useless. They were weightless, and were about to fall, plunging down together, a ball of clutching limbs.

His mouth was open. He felt the air in his throat and knew nothing could stop him yelling as they fell. He screwed up his eyes as they paused at the top of the plunge. But they hung in space. Beneath them, water rushed and boomed, but they did not follow it down. They were above it, suspended.

Slowly, their heads tight together, they looked beyond the edge of the boat. They were still on water. Flat water. They were on a narrow strip of water hanging over space. Tekker looked back and then ahead. They were on a bridge, a single thin span stretched like a bowstring from the top of the waterfall towards a distant shore. And the bridge seemed to be made of water.   .

He brought his gaze back from the giddy drop and tried to make out what supported them. There was a stone kerb on either side and the black posts continued marking the edge, standing at wide intervals, looming up and flicking past as they sped by.

Little by little, fearful of rocking the shallow leaf and sending it careering towards the kerb and over the edge, they sat upright. Kit saw the water glimmering ahead. It made a line of light too thin to hold them.

She clung tighter to Tekker and let the words come out between clenched teeth. 'I know we're going to fall. It's going to crack. It can't hold.'

'I can see the far side.'

'The bridge will break.'

'We're over a pit.' He could see a circular gulf into which the lagoon poured. 'Half way across.'

The thin span of the bridge speared towards the pale lip where the far side of the lagoon slid down, curving smoothly before it flung out spray like a million white fingers that clutched and clutched for the edge but again and again lost their grip and fell away.

The thud and boom from far below grew to drown their words. He put his head alongside hers. 'We're going to hit rough water, Kit.'

He could feel her cheek muscles tighten as she nodded.

The current coming in from the far side would run against them.

'Hang on!'

His shout came as the boat hit choppy waves. It banged into the kerb, and the jolt sent them sideways and they shipped more water.

'We're sinking!' Kit saw the edge of the silvery leaf go under.

'Jump!'

Together they launched themselves at the kerb. Their hands slapped cold stone and they slammed into it flat on their stomachs, winded. Tekker hauled his legs from the water and twisted to see the boat tilt, slip under the broken surface and vanish.

Kit had her cheek against the stone. It was solid, and she dared not raise her head. A movement by Tekker made her bite her lip to prevent a whimper. One slip, and they would be gone.

Tekker eased himself up until he was sitting on the kerb. It was broad. By leaning forward he could just touch both sides.

'Kit,' he said. 'Sit up.'

Very slowly, she curled her legs beneath her and knelt. One of the posts stood not far away.

'Can you make it?' he said, and she crawled ahead of him while the boom from the cataract in the caverns below roared as if to swallow them.

The pillar blocked almost the whole width of the kerb.

'You'll have to stand.' He had to shout against the din, and as she eased herself upright against it she knew, even though she could not hear it, she was sobbing.

'We can walk.' He had come alongside her. 'I'll take the outside.' They squeezed past the pillar and stood with their backs to it. He put his arm around her waist and threaded her arm behind his back, where her fingers clutched his soaking shirt. 'We'll be steady like this.'

They began to move along the wet path, shuffling forward with tiny steps. The black space roared and sucked at them, but he kept talking. 'We're safe if we hold on. We balance each other.' And then, when they stiffened and rocked and were in danger of pulling each other sideways, he began to call the steps . . . left, right, left, right . . . and they marched.

They edged around each pillar as they came to it, clung to steady their breathing, and then marched again. The far lip of the pit gradually came closer.

'We're going to make it, Kit.' But the edge where the lagoon plunged was almost worse than the space at their backs. The water slid silently to meet the roar below but it brought the air with it and a breeze pressed against them as though it wanted to push them over into the sinister flood that now washed against the kerb. Dizziness made her freeze, but he forced her on. 'Keep going!'

The kerb became a path with water on both sides, and when it was flowing past them more gently they went forward in single file.

'It's warmer.' They were her first words since leaving the chasm behind. She stopped. The stone path was just clear of the water and they seemed to stand on the surface of the lagoon in which the glimmering hillside was reflected. 'The heat's coming from there.' She pointed to the shore.

'It needs to be warmer,' he said. 'I'm wet and my feet squelch.'

They sat down and took off their shoes. For a few moments they were silent, resting, and then he said, 'For some reason I feel almost safe out here.'

'It's that.' She nodded towards the slope that spread its glitter around them on the water. 'It's warm.'

'Is it on fire?'

She shook her head.

'It might be burning inside,' he said.

'But it isn't.'

They were sitting cross-legged, side by side, and he glanced at her from the corner of his eye. Her face was bathed in the warm light from the shore and she gazed at it with a calmness he suddenly wanted to disturb. 'Anyway, we haven't far to go,' he said. 'Can't have.'

'Further than you think.'

'You suddenly seem to know a lot.'

She did not answer.

'It was me who got us here in the first place, don't forget. Now you think you know more about it than I do.' All the fears he had been struggling to control came out as anger. 'If it hadn't been for me learning the trick of seeing things, you'd have never known anything about all this.'

Still she gazed ahead, almost ignoring him. 'Those two sisters,' she said, 'they knew about this long before you. Long before Mr Welbeck, even. It's not your property.'

'Great,' he said. 'Marvellous. Big deal. Why isn't everybody here, then? Why isn't it crowded out with people? It should be, according to you.'

Again she did not answer.

'What is all this then? A dream? Or is it a nightmare? Is it all going to fade away?'

'It might,' she said.

'And I suppose Dan will fade away with it.' He stopped. He had said too much. After a moment, he murmured, 'I'm sorry.'

But Kit hardly seemed to have heard. She said, 'There's always something just beyond the edge of things, and sometimes you learn the trick of getting there.'

'It was me who told you that. I got us here.'

'I know,' she said. 'But I'm there now.' It was as

though she had just realized it. She turned towards him. 'Not many manage it, Tekker.'

'There's not many mad enough to try.' Suddenly he was smiling. 'Just two crazy sisters and an old man.'

'And us.'

'And us. You know what I think, Kit?' She shook her head. 'I think we'd never have known about all this if those two sisters hadn't hated each other. They made a crack and we got through.'

'I guessed that ages ago,' she said, and stood up.

'What else have you guessed?'

'You'll see.'

She led the way along the stone path until the growl of the chasm diminished to a murmur and then faded altogether. The lights on the hillside had become clearer.

'It seems to be covered in buildings,' he said. 'Houses.'

'But it's deserted.' She could see lights, yellow and flickering, glinting back from walls and roofs of glass. In places the lights shone directly through walls and doorways, but nowhere was there any movement.

'There's streets,' he said. 'And courtyards, I think.' But a double row of brighter lights rose in the middle of the slope to the crest of the hill where the tower burned among the stars. 'It's too steep for a roadway,' he said. 'I can't make it out.'

'Can't you?' She was laughing at him. 'We'd better get closer. Oh I can't stand these things.' As she spoke she lifted her shoes which she had tied together by their laces and hung round her neck. 'There they go!' She whirled them once around her head and flung them far out across the water. 'Now I feel ready.'

'I don't know what's happened to you all of a sudden, Kit,' he said, 'but I like it.' He was laughing as he flung his own shoes after hers. 'Lead on!'

They ran until the path petered out in shallow water.

Then they splashed on to a shelving beach of stone that soon levelled out in a flat expanse that stretched away out of sight on either side. She pulled up.

'Now can you see?'

The shimmering hillside filled the sky, and from its foot the double row of lamps climbed straight up. Suddenly he saw what they were.

'It's a staircase!' Even though he was looking at it his mind failed to grasp it. 'It's a staircase right into the sky!'

'It goes on for ever!' she cried. 'You can't even see the top!'

21

·

Stella

Long shadows stretched behind them as they ran
barefoot towards the hillside. It was flecked with sparks
like a bonfire that had died down but was still burning
within, and only the track of the vast staircase showed
clearly.

'It's for giants,' Tekker panted as they ran. 'Huge
steps.'

Each rise was marked by lamps on either side, and even
the first was high overhead.

'Idiot.' She was ahead of him. 'They're not single steps
– they're whole flights.'

And then he saw. The first lamps marked a resting
place, a wide landing, and above it was another and
another.

The sight of them stacked one above the other like
hanging balconies reaching to the sky made him slow and
then stop. 'I reckon there's a hundred steps up to that first
place,' he said, 'and then a hundred to the next one.'

'And the next, and the next.' She was alongside him,
but impatient.

'We're going to crawl up that like beetles.'

'And the night's not going to last forever.'

They were running again and the foot of the stairs
seemed to widen as they got nearer. On either side, but
many paces away, rose the walls of buildings that clothed

the slope, some with doorways opening directly on the stairs. They kept to the middle and found the treads so broad that it was like going up a gentle ramp, but by the time they reached the first landing they were breathing heavily, and turned to look back. They were already far above ground.

'I'm only giddy when I look up,' said Kit. The steps were so broad there seemed no danger of falling.

It took them twenty paces to cross the smooth glass to the foot of the next flight. 'At least it rests your climbing muscles,' he said.

'And cools your feet.'

He had forgotten they were running barefoot, but now he felt stripped down, ready for action. No haversack, no shoes. All he had kept was the knife on its cord around his waist. He tried not to grin, but failed.

'All or nothing, Kit,' he said.

She was smoothing her sleeves. 'My shirt's getting dry already.'

'Trust a girl to think of that,' he said. 'Want to borrow a comb?'

She began to climb. 'Some people never take to you, Tekker Begdale. I can see why.'

They found a rhythm, climbing the shallow flights at a steady pace, and then jogging across the flat landings. They put five more flights behind them before they paused to look back. Far beneath, the ground was black and hidden, and already they felt they had floated free of the earth. Up here it was very silent.

Kit spoke in a whisper. 'We're right out in the open, Tekker. Anything could see us.'

Away to each side of them the tall lamps that marked the landing stood in alcoves set back among the houses. They glared with a white light, and the glass platform was shot through with many colours. The edges of the

stairs caught the light and made a silvery cascade against
which they must show clearly.

They searched the stars and listened. Nothing cut
through the night sky, but as they turned to climb the
next flight they angled gradually towards the edge.

'It might be better,' he said, 'if we could climb without
using the stairs. There must be roads up the hill.'

'We'd get lost. We haven't time.' Her voice dropped
even lower as they approached the glass walls that edged
the stairs. None of the buildings was tall, but there were
terraces and angles and doorways and occasionally little
squares opening from the landings as though the staircase
itself was no more than a road running through a glimmering city. And they saw what made the hillside shine
with points of light. Corners and alleyways were lit by
little cups that held flickering flames.

'Like candles,' she said. 'The whole place looks asleep.'
And the silence of the slope wrapped them round as they
climbed higher into the night.

Flight after flight dropped away behind them, but their
legs gradually became heavy and then began to tremble.

'We must rest,' he said. 'Next landing.'

They climbed to the platform and he led her to the
alcove at the side where a great lamp stood in its pool of light.
From its heavy pedestal a twisted stem of bronze
and coloured glass rose to support three huge globes cradled in ornate brackets, and they sat with their backs
against the base.

Kit tilted her face to look up the slope. 'It seems to go
on as far as ever,' she said. The next huge lamp hung
against the sky, and beyond it the others were piled one
above the other until they seemed no bigger than sparks.

Tekker was gazing down the slope to where the globes
now shrank to pinpricks below. They seemed to be strung
out in space, supported on nothing and, as he moved his

head, the string of lights sagged and dipped. He straightened, giddily. He had almost fallen asleep.

'Kit.' Her head was back against the pedestal and her eyes were closed. 'Kit!' He was reaching to touch her shoulder when he paused. Something that had been constantly in the back of his mind stirred. He listened, and heard what he had been waiting for. Wingbeats.

He shook her. 'They're coming!' Instantly she was awake, her head twisting as she searched. 'Out there. Listen.'

He pointed to the deep blackness far below. A sigh reached them, died, then came again. Wings pulsed, but they could see nothing.

'How many?' she said.

They could not tell, nor even how far away. Kit glanced up at the three bright globes that put them in a pool of light. 'They'll see us.'

She began to move away but he pulled her back to the base of the twisted column. 'Stay still. It's movement they see.'

Standing rigidly in the bright light they strained their eyes to penetrate the blackness. A sudden distant whistle in the air and a quick beating made them start. Then there was a long, grating slide, and silence.

Kit's heart thumped in her ears as she strove to listen. Nothing reached her and she turned to Tekker. He shook his head. 'It must have landed,' he said.

'Where?' She searched wildly.

'Down there somewhere.' He pointed down into the blackness. There was nothing. And then, against the silver glint of the stars far below, a black speck showed. They stopped breathing. No sound reached them, but the speck was moving. Very slowly it was putting the blackness behind it as it rose.

Tekker glanced up. The lamps still dwindled to

nothingness above, and the speck was coming on smoothly. They would never win a race. His brain worked clearly and fast.

'We can't go out on the stairs,' he said. 'It'll see us. We've got to risk the houses.'

They slid back behind the pedestal. There were walls of green and amber in a semicircle broken only by a single gap that led into a narrow alleyway. They ran for it.

Tekker plunged ahead of her into the narrow slot. Light reflected through the walls flecked them with green and blue as they ran but the path was level and smooth and their bare feet made little sound.

Beyond the end of the passage he saw a yellow light flicker, and he slowed, creeping towards the opening. She caught up with him and they eased themselves to the corner and looked out.

A flame, dancing in a cup high on the corner of the house, lit a small square. Even in the dim light, colours glowed in walls and doorways. The whole square shimmered dimly, one house of blue deepening within to purple, and another made of clear glass but, behind its wall, hung with peacock curtains that reached from roof to floor. Directly opposite them was a house in three tiers showing red corridors and distant, warm depths. Tekker gazed in and through it.

'There's a light behind,' he whispered. 'There must be a way through.'

'Wait!' Kit hung back. 'I want to watch.' The flame guttered and flared, and made shadows move behind the red walls.

He glanced back. The speck on the stairs would be closer. 'We've got to go. Now.' He stepped forward but she snatched at his shirt.

'Look!'

The flare had steadied, but within the house something

continued to move. On the ground floor, changing shape as it was caught and mirrored in smooth walls, a shadow flitted from room to room. Even in the red, dim light they could see it was pale, and at every shift it came nearer.

He was still half into the square and his head jerked, seeking an escape. There was only one way. In the far corner, marked by the flame, another narrow alleyway led up the mountainside. But he had seen it too late. The shape, rippling past the last layer of glass, had found an opening. It came out and faced them across the square.

'It's a woman!' Kit's gasp echoed and died.

The flame guttered, dimming, but it showed the face. It had him shrinking back, ready to run.

Kit saw everything. The dark fringe and the straight hair cut short against the smooth cheeks. The small mouth and button nose of Ma Grist. But not her.

Kit's cry rang out. 'Stella!'

The woman was young but her dress was in a style of long ago. It made a straight line from shoulder to knee, and her arms were bare. She smiled, and Kit was certain.

'We've found her!' She spun to Tekker and tried to pull him forward, but still he hung back. 'John Welbeck's Stella – can't you see!'

The image of the stout woman in brown would not leave him.

'The disc!' Kit hauled at him. 'Give her the disc!'

The woman, even though the width of the square separated them, raised a hand as though she expected to be given it. Then her eyes rested on Tekker, and she saw his doubt. Her arm fell and she stood quite still with her hands clasped loosely in front of her. She was content that he should judge. It was then that his doubts melted. A false Stella would have tried to persuade him. Suddenly he was digging in his pocket for the pouch.

'Quick!' Kit cried and tugged him with her into the open.

He had the pouch in his hand and was pulling the drawstrings wide when a slight movement in Stella's head checked him. Her hair swung against her cheek as she turned. She was listening.

The silence was intense. It held them rigid. And then they heard it. A soft footfall. It came from the mouth of the passage opposite. The flame flickered but showed nothing. The soft pad of a foot again, but Tekker had dashed ahead and Stella was coming to meet him.

They were too late. Too much space lay between them when the long skull showed under the light. The neck arched from the black shoulders, and the stiff crest stood upright over the black eye sockets as it strode out. They were cut off.

Tekker had the disc in his grasp. He held it high for Stella to see, and drew back his arm to throw. But bristles scratched stone and black limbs thrust the long body between them. He had missed the chance.

It was then that Stella spoke. Her voice was not loud, but it was clear in his head. 'Turn the disc. Turn it.'

His fingers fumbled at its edge as the Horsehead came for him.

22

·

Dan

The skull dipped for him. He saw hairline cracks in the bone, like veins, and his fingers stiffened on the disc. It would not turn.

A long arm sliced down and he lunged sideways. But too late. It hit his shoulder and he staggered. A shock of pain loosened his grip and it was then, twisting against his palms, that the disc began to move. It turned, but he was on his knees and the pale shape was above him, looking down.

'Tekker!' He heard Kit's cry and felt her hands under his arms, helping him to his feet, but he struggled free. The danger was still there.

The thin face looked at him. Dark eye sockets and pale bone. It had come down on a level with him, and he heard it breathing.

He thrust back, trying to take Kit with him, but she resisted.

'No!' He heard her voice. 'It's all right! We've come back. We're on the road. Can't you see?'

All he saw was the crouching figure in front of him. Then a voice came from it.

'Is the young man hurt?'

'No,' said Kit. 'I don't think so.'

The head bowed, and then Tekker saw. They were in the road outside Kit's house and John Welbeck stood in

front of them. The white head was his, and it was his stick
that had come down and caught his shoulder.

'I struck at you, young man.' The pale, stern face was
lifted. 'You appeared so suddenly I mistook you.' He had
to draw in his breath. 'I took you for an enemy.'

Tekker was bewildered. They were in the wrong place.
They should be far out in the fens, not here. And the old
man had been guarded by Ma Grist, waiting for him to
die, believing he still had the disc.

'What happened?' he said. 'How did you get away?'

'She found out.' John Welbeck's head came up but he
still had to rest on his stick with both hands. 'Her creatures saw you out there.' He nodded towards the flat fens.
'And then she knew you had the disc.'

'So she left you.' Kit was ahead of him. 'She let you go.'

'She took her guards and went away. I was no longer
any danger to her.' He was a weak old man but he gestured suddenly with his stick towards the house and his
voice snapped. 'I came to see the boy. I came to help.'

Kit's heart thudded as though it was its last beat. Dan.
His window was lit but the rest of the house was in
darkness. Suddenly she knew.

'It was Stella who got us here!' She was leaning
forward, staring into Tekker's eyes, forcing him to see.
'We reached her. She almost touched the disc. That
helped her. She sent us back. To Dan.'

She turned to run, but the old man's voice stopped her.
'Stella. I saw her.' He was dazed. 'She seemed to stand in
that doorway. She looked at me.'

'So it's not too late!' Kit began to move but the old man
was too quick for her. His cold fingers closed on her wrist.

'She's gone.' In the shadow of his brows his eyes were
hard. 'They came for her. Those creatures. They came
between us. That's why I struck out.'

'Where is she? Where did she go?'

'She vanished. I lost her.'

'I'll find her!' Kit broke free and was running barefoot with Tekker towards the house. Behind him, he heard the old voice say, 'It's too late, son. She's gone for good.'

Kit had pushed at the front door. It was open. The stairs were in darkness, but suddenly a door opened above and in the shaft of light she saw her father.

'How is he?' The words started from her as she climbed. 'How's Dan?'

Her father had switched on the light and was coming down fast, his face thin and tense. 'In a moment,' he said. 'In a moment.' He pushed past her and snatched up the phone on the hall table.

He was dialling as she pushed open the door of Dan's room. Her mother was sitting by the bed where the single light showed Dan lying as though asleep. She heard Kit come in, but did not turn away from the bed.

'Are they coming?' her mother said.

Kit went closer and stood behind her, looking down at Dan.

'Are they?' Her mother repeated the question and then saw who it was. 'Your father's phoning the doctor,' she said. 'Hadn't you better go back to bed?' She had not even noticed Kit's clothes.

'Mum. What's happening?'

'Nothing, my love. We just think somebody ought to have a look at Dan.'

'He's worse, Mum. He's much worse, isn't he?'

Her mother did not answer but leant forward to smooth Dan's fair hair against his brow. 'He's so cold,' she said, and tucked the blankets closer to his chin.

Tekker came into the room, and as he did so Kit's mother turned sharply. 'Oh it's you,' she said, but her eyes were too filled with worry to think it strange. 'Has he got through?'

'I think so.' He could hear Kit's father talking in the hall.

'They've got to hurry. He's got to make them hurry.' She wrenched herself away from the bed and went with quick steps across the room and out, leaving them standing by the bedside.

Dan's breathing was so gentle Kit could barely hear it. His face was utterly calm, and his hair was neat.

'Oh Dan!' It was little more than a sob that escaped from her. 'Don't look like that.' His cheeks had never been so smooth or so white.

Tekker reached for Kit's hand and realized he was still clutching the disc. Too late for this. Too late for anything. He was opening his fingers when Dan's eyelids moved. They did not open, but a frown put a fold between his eyebrows.

'Dan!' She leant forward. 'Can you hear me!'

His lips fell open as though to breathe, but then they moved and formed words it was almost impossible to hear. 'I saw her. Stella. Saw her.'

'Where?'

He frowned again. The question was irrelevant. 'Saw her. She said . . .' A shudder deepened the lines between his eyes. Exhaustion was claiming him. They leant closer. One soft breath, and then his lips moved again. 'Said climb . . . climb.'

His mouth stayed open. They both bent low listening for his breath. It was there, but as faint as a moth's wing. And then, over the rooftop, a rushing in the air blotted it out.

23

.

At the Top of the Sky

The rush in the air ceased, and as silence gasped around the house Kit raised her head. Her eyes were wide and her mouth was open. She was afraid, but not of the wingbeats over the rooftop.

'He can't hear me any more!' The knowledge seemed to startle her. 'Dan can't hear me!'

Dan's head, smooth and secret, lay still as though it was being exhibited on the pillow, and Tekker had to force his stiff limbs to move from the bedside.

'He said climb.' He drew Kit with him. 'He saw Stella. She said climb.'

Kit did not seem to hear him. He shook her arm. 'They're coming back. They'll be here any second. We've got to climb.' He heard the telephone being put down in the hall, and the faint jangle reached her. She gave a little shake of the head and tugged at him to follow her.

They went swiftly across the landing just as her parents turned away from the telephone in the hall below. In the shadows she opened a door and he heard her bare feet running up wooden stairs. He followed, fumbling his way through the darkness to where a dim outline of a sloping window in the roof showed him uncarpeted floorboards.

'It's the attic,' she said.

'I know.' He had heard Dan talk about it.

'We can't climb any further. Turn the disc.'

It was still in his hand. He gave her the pouch and she held it open, ready. Whatever happened now, there would be no going back.

'Ready?'

She nodded. Quickly, he turned the disc on his palm, slid it into the pouch and she pulled the drawstrings and thrust it into her pocket before either of them raised their heads.

They stood in a shimmer of faint light. The floor had vanished and they were suspended in space, treading on no more than shadows. They were in a room of glass and beneath them they could see other floors descending mistily in a long shaft. They turned delicately for fear of falling and looked down through a slant of walls to where a little flame flickered in what seemed an open space.

'It's the square,' he said. 'Where we saw Stella.' They had climbed right through the building where she had appeared.

Kit was already moving, sliding her bare feet gingerly across the invisible glass towards a wall filled with dim, transparent colours. She could see a doorway. There was a roof above them hazily obscuring the stars, and the door itself was visible only because a light somewhere outside glowed through its smoky thickness. She pushed, and without a sound it swung open.

A narrow walkway, sparkling faintly, led across rooftops, becoming invisible before it reached the line of climbing lamps that marked the stairs.

'We're higher than before,' she whispered.

Tekker looked up. For the first time he could see the pinnacle, and below them the steep slope fell away glimmering into nothingness. They were close to the roof of the night.

'She got us this far,' said Kit. 'She can't do any more.'

Tekker was studying the climb. Once they had reached

he stairs it was going to be a straight dash for the top.
But it's not going to be that easy,' he said.

'What do you mean?'

'We've seen her. But something comes between.
Always.'

'Not this time. Not now. If we move fast.'

As they stepped out he was looking down to make sure
that the cord which held his knife was still around his
waist, and when Kit stopped suddenly he stumbled into
her.

'There's something up there!' She held him still.

From far overhead there came a long sigh in the sky.
They knew what to expect and waited for it. A rustling
creak and then the wings bit the air again. A moment
later and a shape flickered across the lights near the pinnacle and vanished, but already they were running along
the flimsy gangway.

'Only one,' he said. 'A patrol. And it can't land up
there.'

But Kit's mind was racing as she ran. A Horsehead had
been climbing after them when they left the stairs.
Another had almost touched them as they turned the
disc. There could be more.

On bare feet, almost soundlessly, they skimmed the
rooftops and slowed only when the tall lamp standard
above with its triple globes loomed close. Panting, they
came out on to the platform and crept towards its base. It
was then that real giddiness took hold of Kit and had her
clutching at the pedestal. They were far higher than
before. The stairs fell away beneath them, dwindling to
the narrowness of a single rod of light and resting on a
point so distant she felt the whole structure heeling
against the sky.

'We can make it.' He walked forward, and the sight of
him standing against the stars, in space, made her turn

away and cling tighter to the twisted bronze. She felt sick.
She could not go on.

'Hell!' he said.

His voice was not loud but it put a new fear into her.
'What is it?'

'I'm not sure.' He beckoned her and she left the pedestal
and edged forward, keeping her eyes fixed on him. But he
was gazing below, and when she reached him she twined
her fingers in the sleeve of his shirt and tilted her head to
look down.

'There's more than one,' he said. 'A lot more.' Dots
speckled the band of light far below. 'And they're coming
fast.'

They turned together on the glass platform and ran for
the stairs. As they leapt higher and higher her giddiness
slid away, forgotten. They were in a race.

They reached a landing. 'Twenty!' he called as they ran
across it. 'About twenty more.'

They thrust the cold glass behind them, sucking at the
thin air as the next lamps swayed nearer, and then the next.

'Steeper.' She was fighting for breath. 'They're steeper.'

And the glimmer of houses had fallen behind. The staircase rose beyond the hill. It held itself clear of the slope on
vast columns, climbing straight into the sky.

They came to another level and had to pause, gasping.
Holding to each other, they looked down. Tekker watched
the shadow rippling upwards towards them and forced
himself to calculate.

No single Horsehead could yet be picked out. 'They're
still a long way off, Kit.' He wiped sweat away from his eyes
and looked up. 'We've got time.'

She had risked raising her eyes to look outwards. It was
still the middle of the night and the land was black. Dar
was out there somewhere. The thought of his thin, pale face
had her twisting away and running.

'He said climb!' she cried. 'Climb!'

Ten more flights, a gasping pause, then five more. Their steps were uncertain and sometimes they reeled and the glass above became filmy and seemed to curve back over them as though to throw them off and drop them down through the swaying, silent sky.

'Stop.' He could hardly speak. His shirt clung to him. 'Rest. Must rest.' He sagged to his knees and, on all fours, looked back. Once again he calculated. 'Minutes. We've got minutes, Kit. And only three flights to go.'

She had flung herself flat and lay spreadeagled, gazing up as her chest heaved in the thin air. Three flights. She could see the top. Or almost. No lamps marked it. The lamps ended at the foot of the final flight, and the last hundred steps shimmered into the stars and were lost.

A star winked and went out. Then another.

'Tekker!' Her whisper brought him round. 'She's there!' A small figure blotted out the stars. 'We've found her!'

And for the first time nothing lay between them and Stella. They were on their feet, arms lifted, and their mouths were open to cry out when the tiny figure itself raised an arm. But not in greeting. It was pointing out into the sky beyond them, urgently stabbing with a pale arm.

They had begun to climb, but now they turned on the stairs to look where she pointed. What they saw was sailing silently like a black boat in the twinkling sea of the stars. Then the lazy lift of its wings sent out a sigh like waves on a beach.

It was distant. Perhaps they were still unseen. In a flicker of pale skirts the figure above vanished, and together they were running for the lamp at the stairs' edge. The full glare was on them and the hiss of wings chased them as they slithered to a halt behind the pedestal. They looked back and up.

It came so fast that for a moment it seemed silent.

Straight for the stairs. Then a clap of wings like thunder shuddered the night and it hung just clear of the last landing above, carving great shadows on the stairs as it scooped the air.

It could not hold like that for along. They saw it stagger as it battered the air, then drop. They heard the clash and scrape of its keel as it slewed on the level and stopped with its snout pointing down the stairs.

It was two flights above them, but it was enormous. Its wings almost touched lamps on either side and at its centre the long bone head that rose above the hump of its body seemed small. The head nodded like a horse, and the long legs stepped clear.

'It's going to climb.' Tekker breathed the words as the Horsehead turned its back. 'When it goes, we move.' His brain was working it out. The flying machine had come down only with great difficulty. No others would land above them. One to beat.

But at his side Kit was shrinking back, trembling. She had seen another figure come from the body of the flying machine and stand in its shadow. It was small, almost squat, and brown. She saw the glint of Ma Grist's spectacles as she tilted her head to gaze down the endless fall of the stairs.

Tekker began to move but Kit snatched at him as the head in its tight brown hat turned away and Ma Grist's figure moved under the arch of one tilted wing.

'She hasn't seen us,' he whispered.

Kit edged further round the pedestal. 'But she knows we're here somewhere. She'll wait.'

Tekker had seen a movement. 'They're climbing.'

First the dumpy figure in brown showed against the glint of glass and then the spidery limbs and dipping head followed. Their progress was slow, and only at the top did they turn to look down. They stood for a long minute, and then the pale head and the spark of spectacles moved out of sight and Tekker was running.

'Keep behind me!' That way they would make one target from above if anything should linger in the black machine.

They sped up the first flight, and were mounting the second when he thought he had a glimpse of movement at the very top.

'Faster!'

Their aching limbs thrust them towards the spread of black wings. It crouched like a great flying beetle, humped in the centre where its jaws waited. Tekker reached the landing and flung himself forward. He staggered and had just time to see Kit run for shelter under the black tent of one wing when he hit the front of the machine and fell. His hands slipped on skin as clammy as cold leather, and he lay half in and half out of a gaping opening.

'Stay still!' Her voice reached him through the skin, and he lay where he was.

The stairs were silent. No noise yet reached them from the rising tide below, and Kit moved in the musty shadow of the wing to look up.

'It's all right.' Her whisper came to him. 'I can't see anything at the top.'

He was face down in the bottom of the machine. His cheeks could feel ribs against the leathery skin, and he raised his head to see a structure of spars and struts stretching back into the hollow shadow of its body. He rolled on to one elbow and reached for a thin crossbar to help him up. It did not take his weight. Instead, it slid down towards him and the whole machine lurched. He heard an urgent shuffle from Kit and let go. The bar slid away from him, and all around him a framework of jointed rods slid back into place as smoothly as oil and the machine righted itself.

He eased himself backwards, touching nothing except the skin, and Kit helped him out. She was trembling.

'The whole wing moved,' she said. 'It came down over me. I thought it was alive.'

'No.' He was gazing into the mesh of rods and hardly noticed her fear. 'I did it. I just pulled it in one place and everything else shifted.' He saw the thin yellow crossbar he had moved. Its end was knuckled to others that led back towards the wing root, and there was a kind of cradle that could have been a seat, and a footrest. In the same glance he saw where claws or hands could reach and how the wings could move with them. A dank, musty smell came from it like ruined churches where bats hung, yet it was delicately balanced, easy to move. He saw it all. It all fitted, and then Kit tugged at him.

Together they went under the arch of the wing and looked up the last flight. The edges of the treads glinted and ended against the sky. Nothing showed at the top.

'They've reached her first,' said Kit. 'All they've got to do is wait for us to come to them.' She stood barefoot, one sleeve hanging loose, and felt all hope flood away. She was small and useless, and her mind ran home, far away and safe – and suddenly she saw Dan. Her blood surged again and she found herself speaking. 'But there's one thing they don't know.'

'What's that?'

'They don't know which one of us has got this.' She had the pouch in her hand. 'We have to split up. One of us might get through.'

And one of us might not. Tekker felt the touch of despair. They would die, like Dan.

'You go that way.' She pointed to one side of the stairs. 'I'll go this.'

He nodded, but his fingers were stiff as he fumbled at the lanyard around his waist.

'Tekker.' She had seen his reluctance and was questioning him. They gazed steadily for a long moment and suddenly, from nothing, they grinned at each other like murder. Fury beyond fear flashed through them, and he opened the knife blade.

'I go first,' he said. 'You have the disc. When I draw them, you find her.'

Then he was loping away, slanting up the stairs. He reached the balustrade. It was no more than waist height, but it was as much cover as he would get. He paused to loop the free end of the lanyard around his hand, took a fresh grip on the knife and waved to her to start out.

He saw her leave the shelter of the black wing and then he began the last of the climb.

Four steps above him the balustrade gave out, jutting just clear of the last step against a thick scatter of stars. He could not see what lay beyond, but a sound reached him. A faint whisper. He froze. Then a murmur. Voices.

He eased himself up one more step and looked over the edge.

'The boy. Just leave the boy.'

Stella. A great circle of glass reflected the stars. She stood far back, near the edge, so distant she was like a doll, her black hair tight to her head, but across the glass her voice was clear.

'Let the boy live through the night and you may have all of this.' She made a tiny movement with both hands at her sides, but it meant the towering stairs, the palace and everything beyond.

'What use is this to me?' The squat brown figure had her back to him. At her side, its crest bristling against the stars, stood the Horsehead. 'What good did all this do for you?'

'John Welbeck saw it.'

'Across the desert he saw it!' The sister's voice bit the cold air. 'My desert kept him from it.'

He saw Stella bow her head. 'It doesn't matter now. Just save the boy.'

'The boy! Who cares about the boy!'

And Tekker climbed to the top and tapped his knife blade on the glass floor.

Together, the heads jerked his way, and then the brown sleeve came up, pointing, releasing her creature at him. It came fast, and Tekker let the knife fall to the length of its cord. He swung it around his head and with all the force in his lungs yelled, 'Now!'

From the corner of his eye he saw a scurry as Kit climbed, and then the long skull filled the sky. An arm reached and he scythed at it. The knife hissed and a scrap of hair flew, but still it came. He ran for open space.

Kit reached the platform. There was no/parapet, and the wide circle of glass hung in the sky like the skin of a bubble. Across it, she saw two figures, side by side.

'Stella!' Her feet as she ran barely touched. 'Stella!' The black hair swung her way, but the brown hat also turned.

Tekker had his back to space. He swung the blade and lunged. He felt the jerk along the cord as it bit, but he lost the arc and the knife clattered uselessly down.

Kit flung the pouch away and held the disc as she leapt forward. Stella began to reach.

The Horsehead towered over him as he dipped for the knife. He scooped it at the bottom of his crouch and rose to meet the ragged snout as it carved the sky above him and came down. He was upright and swaying back. The skull sliced air along his arm and chest and then, like a bullfighter, he had the knife in both hands above his head and was leaning forward, plunging down. The blade caught bone and cracked it open. He heaved back to strike again but it held fast, wedged tight. The bristled neck shuddered, the skull shook once, and the knife was torn from his fingers. He leapt over a sliding arm and ran.

The sisters stood side by side, and Kit was in front of them. As he ran he saw her thrust the disc forward. An arm in a brown sleeve swung up and snatched, but Stella was quicker. Her hand touched Kit's and the disc was in Stella's palm.

They had done it. In the roof of the night sky he slowed and stood beside Kit. They were on invisible glass, and an enormous silence spread outwards and took in all the black land far beneath. Then Stella's voice said quietly, 'It is almost dawn.'

Kit was panting. In the top of her lungs she found enough breath for a single word. 'Dan?' she asked.

Stella smiled. 'I shall see him soon. He is safe.'

'Not yet!' Under the brim of the brown hat the small features were bunched together in the hard flesh. 'The boy is mine!'

The sisters faced each other. The same small, curved mouth, and eyelids that moved slowly over green eyes. Stella said, 'It is over.'

'Not yet, sister.' The small, round glasses threw sparks of light into the green eyes. 'The dawn is yours, but the night is mine.' Stella began to swing away, but a plump hand shot out and thick fingers locked on her wrist. 'I hold you till the sun rises.'

Stella did not struggle. She spoke to Kit. 'She has more strength than I till dawn. But Dan is safe. I have seen him.'

The short laugh was bitter and triumphant. 'You shall have your John Welbeck, sister, but it will give you little joy. The boy will not be there to see it. I can reach him!' Her head swivelled and they followed her gaze to the long shape of the Horsehead lying at the platform's edge. 'My little friend will fly to him.'

Tekker cried out. 'I've killed it! It's dead!'

The head under the close brown hat shook slowly. 'Son,' said the shrill voice, 'you can't kill Death.' And her free hand was extended towards the Horsehead and her lips coaxed it as though it was a dog.

'Don't!' It was Stella's voice. 'You can have everything, but save the boy!'

Her sister, one hand clamped to Stella's wrist, paid no heed. Her lips continued to coax and, as they watched, the long head moved and its jagged muzzle scratched along the glass. 'Come on, my beauty! Come on, my little darling!' The head came up, and oily bristles swept the glass. 'Up you get!'

It stood.

'Now fly for your mother. Seek him out!'

From the front of the skull the knife handle jutted, and the lanyard swung.

'Fly!' she shrieked, and Tekker jerked round. Stella's eyes were on Kit. He saw pity and hopelessness, and then the shriek came again. 'Fly!'

24

·

The Horsehead Rides

'Fly!'

The order was screeched at the Horsehead. It stirred.
Tekker spun, taking Kit with him, and ran for the platform's edge.

'The machine!' He was shouting as they raced for the
top of the stairs. 'We can wreck it!'

He glanced back. The Horsehead had swayed to its feet
and was already taking the first step.

Kit was a pace behind him as he went over the edge,
then the stairs dropped away beneath her, down through
the night and she reeled as vertigo seemed to tip her into
space. She was sagging to clutch the glass and hang on in
the spinning night when his voice came back to her.

'Faster, Kit!'

Trembling, half crouching, she raised her head.
Beyond him, an army was climbing. She could see the
pale heads, the black dots of eye sockets, and the spider
legs hooking their way from step to step, coming fast.
Then bristles brushed glass behind her, and she stood and
launched herself after him. She leapt, two steps at a time,
gulping air, plunging down and knowing that all the time
a thin shriek streamed from her.

He was alongside the body of the machine, heaving.
She leapt the last two steps and ran across the glass to
where the fan of the tail rested. It was skin on a thin

framework. She put both hands to its cold edge and lifted. A shudder went through the whole machine, a wingtip scraped glass and then the shudder rippled back towards them and its weight bore them down. They heaved again. The wingtip scraped a few inches then slid back.

'It's no good!' he cried. Even if they got it over the top step it would lurch and rest, undamaged.

'Try again!' She levered wildly at the hidden spars, trying to break something.

'No!' He held her arm. 'Waste of time.' He glanced upwards. A bristled crest showed. 'Kit, there's one thing.' They faced each other, quite still for one fragment of time, and she knew what he would say. 'We can crash it.'

He saw her hard little smile as she nodded. 'Or fly,' she said.

They ran under the tunnel of the wing, along the boat shape of the machine's body and clambered in at its open front. The cradle, a wickerwork seat, was wide enough for both of them and their bare feet just reached the cold footbar. On either side there was a thin wooden handle among the mesh of struts.

'Are we strong enough?' Her arm went around his waist as she reached forward to the rod on her side.

'We'll soon find out.' His arm was tight around her, and the rigid footbar dug into their insteps as they leant forward and each grasped a handle.

'Together,' he said. 'Lift!'

His right arm went up and, with her left arm, she followed his movement. A network of struts alongside them moved like oil, and over the edge of the bodywork she saw the whole wing lift against the stars. Then a violent lurch flung them sideways. The machine had tilted Tekker's way.

'Down!' he said. 'Bring your arm down!'

Together they brought their arms level. The wings

thudded down and slid on the glass, and the machine righted itself.

They sat still, gasping, and saw the first ragged row of swaying heads reach the landing below.

'We didn't go forward!' she said. 'We can't make it fly!'

'We've got to reach.' Tekker's mind was out along the wings, fingering the air. 'Reach and pull back.' He glanced at her. 'Ready?'

She nodded.

'Now!' he yelled and lunged forward so swiftly her head banged into his shoulder. But her arm matched his and she saw both wings rise and swing forward. 'And heave!'

Before the machine had time to tilt they flung themselves back into the seat and hauled back. The wings went with them, carving a hollow in the night air so swiftly that the rush of sound came later. And the machine slid forward. But not fast enough. He knew it. And they were turning sideways.

'Together!' he yelled. 'Now!'

They reached until they were almost falling through the open front, and the machine was skidding to a halt. The grating of its keel hid the footfalls as the Horsehead came up behind. Its claws dug into the skin of the bodywork.

'Back!' They heaved and, like a wounded bird, the wings beat the glass and the machine pushed itself to the edge. But still not fast enough to fly. Its keel crashed on to the first step and they slewed further sideways.

'Hold still!' He saw what to do. He tightened his grip around her waist, holding her to the back of the seat, and with his other arm reached forward. He twisted the grip and saw the wing arch itself. He hauled back. The wing scooped air and the open mouth swung to face down the slope. But still they plunged from step to step, jolting and crashing to the sea of bone and blank sockets rising to meet them.

'Together, Kit. Now!'

Their arms went out and forward and they stood on the footrest like a single person. She saw his hand twist and she did the same.

'Heave!'

With all their force they pulled back and down. The whole framework thudded on a step, rose shuddering, but could not hold itself and crashed down. They hauled again. Again it lifted, staggered and fell. They braced themselves for the jolt, but it did not come. They slid inches clear of the steps, falling free.

They slid in silence. But then the air was rushing past their faces and pressing against their chests and suddenly, without a word, they knew how to ride it.

Arms wide. The wings spread, skimming the stairs, but still going down, plunging like a wave. And the Horseheads were a beach of bone.

The thrum in the wings reached their fingers. Still not fast enough. The first skull glared in front of them. They could not clear it. The open edge in front of their feet hit it. There was a crack and splinters of bone fell around the footrest. Then they were in a foam of bone and thin, thrashing limbs, ploughing a furrow.

They twisted their wrists and the throbbing wings tilted up, flattened in the sudden push of air and their keel slid free.

The lamps dropped suddenly away. They were out and clear. Flying.

Together they reached forward and pulled back, rowing themselves into space. Then they held their arms wide, and sailed.

Tekker felt Kit's fingers digging hard into the soft flesh beneath his ribs and he turned his head to face her.

'We can fly.' He was grinning. 'We did it!'

They soared against the stars until the breeze lessened

against their cheeks. 'Turn,' she said. 'We've got to find out where we are.'

He watched her dip her wing and he flattened his own out against the sky as they went in a curve that brought the glittering stairs in front of them. They drifted, feathering their wingtips, searching the dim platform at the top for a glimpse of Stella. They could see nothing there, but the bright highway of the stairs was scattered with broken swathes of black dots, some still moving.

'We can't land there,' he said. 'We've got to go down. Find the desert.'

'It's almost dawn.' She looked into the distance as they hung in the top of the curve. 'You can see the palace.' It spread out below in a crust of silver except where the chasm gaped, swallowing the vast waterfall. 'Can you hear it?'

'Too far,' he said. The silence was absolute. 'But I can see the bridge.' It was stretched like a thread over the gaping blackness.

They rocked gently and the breeze sighed once more over the wings as they slid from the peak of their flight. Kit was still twisting, searching for landmarks along the pale line of the horizon, when from the corner of her eye she saw movement. A ripple in the leather fabric behind her shoulder. She turned to examine it. Not leather. It was hard and hooked. A black claw. She wrenched her head backwards, mouth open, neck exposed, and the Horsehead skull looked down at her.

She screamed and lunged forward, taking Tekker with her. He caught one glimpse of his knife jutting from the head and the lanyard swinging in front of the sickly, dead mask and then, as their arms bent, the wings folded and they plunged.

The wind flattened their cheeks and choked them but they rolled their heads, one against the other, and looked down. The stars spun and the bright stairs flicked past in a flash of white fire, but the Horsehead, digging deep with both claws, rode at their backs just out of reach. Out of reach. Suddenly Tekker's mind became cold and clear.

'Kit!' Even though his head was pressed against hers he had to shout against the scream of the wind. He felt her nod. 'The bridge! Under it!'

They had slipped from the seat but their fingers clung to the back of it. They perched on the footrest over the open front, falling headlong with the wings streamed back, guiding the plunge.

No words. They knew what to do. For long seconds the black pit yawned slowly open as the wind shrieked and shut their eyes and stopped their breath. They looked back. The Horsehead clung, pressed down by the wind, but crouching, ready.

They turned away. While the air tore at them they were safe. And the pit gaped suddenly wide. They were at its lip when his yell came.

'Now!'

They flung their arms wide. The wings cracked open. A jarring lurch as somewhere a strut broke. But the wings bit. They levelled. The bridge was across their track.

'Keep down!'

His shout was choked by the force that thrust them into the floor of the machine. Their muscles tore as they held their arms wide, but as the boom from the depths drowned the whistle of the straining wings, his voice was chanting steadily, 'Wait . . . Wait . . . Wait.' A pause. 'Now!'

They twisted their wrists. The machine lurched into a dip. The stonework hurled itself at them and they turned to shield themselves from the crash.

Through the slits of their eyes they saw it happen. The edge of the bridge swung like a hammer at the skull. The nife drove home. They heard bone rend and crack open nd the mass of bristle, bone and broken claw was swept ff.

Then the machine was slithering against the underside f the stone span, struts breaking, leather skin tearing, nd they fell.

The thundering echo came from the depths to pull hem down. Walls of water streaked by, racing them as hey plunged. They arched their arms without hope in the roken machine, but as they did so the tattered wings ased themselves outwards, and held.

They spiralled. Slowly and painfully they pushed hemselves upright in the framework. Then, just clear of he walls of sheer water, they began to beat their way pwards.

25

•

Out of the Maze

They came up from the pit on wings that creaked and
groaned, and they fought to gain height, crossing the
lagoon. Very gradually they limped upwards, hauling
themselves towards the sky, but rocking and dipping in
the cold air.

'I can't go on.' Kit's muscles were quivering as her
strength began to give out. 'I've got to rest.'

They took one long pull then slumped like oarsmen
with their blades feathered. By twisting their wrists they
steadied the glide on the edge of stalling, and looked
down. The stars had begun to pale and dissolve, but the
sun did not yet show and the landscape that had opened
out beneath them was as grey as ice.

'It's like a maze.' Tekker still struggled for breath. 'A
glass maze.'

They saw the shape of the palace for the first time.
Buildings spread outwards in a vast circle to the outer
wall, and roads and paths cut through in every direction.

Somewhere behind them the stairs rose, but they
searched for a way out towards the cliff and the desert.

Then Kit saw the dome where they had entered, and
they hauled again, rowing steadily towards it. The dome
slid by and as they crossed the wall they glimpsed the
mirror that it made for the moat and the dark plain of
moss, but they were losing height.

'We've got to go higher,' he said. 'There's the cliff.'

Kit looked out along the wing on her side of the black craft as she reached forward in time with Tekker and pulled back. 'It's torn,' she said. 'Big pieces are flapping.'

'And I've got a broken spar.' He could feel it grind, and occasionally the wingroot lurched. He coaxed another gulp of air, and the keel lifted slightly. 'I don't think we can last much longer.'

She did not reply. Beneath them the moss and marsh eased past too slowly, and the wall of the cliff seemed always to step back, further away. Somewhere beyond it Dan lay. Had he survived the long night?

'Faster,' she said. 'We've got to risk it.'

'Hold tight, then.' His arm around her waist gripped hard, and she bunched his shirt in her fist as they leant forward until they were half out of the open front. 'Now back.' The wings swept back and a rush of cold air squeezed tears from her eyes.

Without talking now, in time, they rowed themselves up through the air to the clifftop and skimmed the boulders just as the first light lay on the land.

They were low. A tree clipped their keel and they rocked. They held steady. A house sped for them. They pulled, and it flicked beneath them.

There was no desert. 'We're through!' she cried.

'But where are we?' They were twice house-height and flying faster, but lurching as weakened spars strained. Then he saw the railway. 'And there's the road.' He nodded towards it and they banked to fly parallel to it over the flat land.

Only the signalman, in his box for an early train, saw them. 'Like a great black sheet, it was,' he said later, 'flapping over the land. It must have been ten thousand birds.'

They came in fast and low, heading for the road outside her house.

They had lined it up and were sliding down when a car's headlights sliced suddenly towards them.

'Orchard!' she shouted, and heaved them round.

Tekker's wing dipped. He saw its tip flick an outhouse roof and instinctively he drew back. They straightened but had lost speed. They came up into a stall and it was too late to recover. They held still in the air just above the tree tops, then settled.

He heard branches puncture the skin, and struts crack and then they were tipped forward and were hanging to the framework just clear of the ground. They lowered themselves to earth. There was enough light to see the machine hanging like a tattered tarpaulin blown there by the gale, but Kit did not once glance at it. She was stumbling and running towards the house.

He saw the car's headlights sweep through the trees and go out. He heard feet crunch on the gravel, then the sound of a door opening, and they reached the house just as the doctor climbed the stairs and went into Dan's bedroom.

They bounded on bare feet after him as he pushed the door open.

Kit's mother and father stood back from the bed. In the shadow their hands were locked and they did not see Kit or Tekker come in. The doctor had pulled the sheets down to Dan's waist and was bending over, pressing the stethoscope to his chest, concentrating. There was no movement in Dan.

Kit went forward, past her mother and father, and reached for the hand that lay limply at Dan's side. Tekker heard her mother gasp and moved to pull her back, but as Kit touched him Dan's head rolled on the pillow, and his eyelids flickered and parted.

For several long seconds the doctor stayed where he was, listening, and then he straightened, the stethoscope hanging around his neck.

Dan frowned and saw Tekker at the foot of his bed. 'I've had a rotten dream, Begdale. I hold you responsible.'

In the sudden surge of activity they found themselves in the background. Kit was trying to dry her eyes on her sleeve.

'Use mine,' said Tekker. He found one ripped cuff dangling and tore it off. He watched the tears come again, quite silently, and make her eyes luminous. He drew her away from the talking, excited figures by the bed. 'We're not finished yet,' he said. 'John Welbeck.'

She nodded, not yet able to speak, and went with him.

The road was cold and rough to their bare feet, but they ran until they stood on the bank above John Welbeck's cottage. Flecks of mist lay waist high in the grey light of the garden, and the dead branches of a tree reached towards the door with twisted fingers. Like a Horsehead. The thought was in their minds when a scraping footstep in the road spun them round.

The road sloped up to the bridge, empty. The scrape came again, and with it the tap of a stick and then, coming towards them over the hump of the bridge, they saw the two figures.

The woman with John Welbeck was smaller than she had seemed at the top of the stairs, but her dress was as pale and her hair was black. They had stopped, waiting, and her arm was linked in his.

Kit and Tekker went up to meet them.

'Young man.' The harsh voice rapped at Tekker. 'You flew over me a moment ago. You were excessively clumsy.' The glint of grey eyes switched suddenly to Kit and he bowed stiffly. 'You put this young lady at risk.'

'We crashed,' said Tekker.

'You're not the first!' He gave a bark of a laugh.

Kit had heard nothing. Her eyes were on the woman. The hair was Stella's, but the face had changed. Rounded. Small mouth and small nose. They belonged with a brown hat.

Kit's bare foot began to slide back, and her mouth opened. Then Stella smiled.

'No need for you to run away,' she said. 'I'm myself.'

'Yes,' said Kit. Stella's smile proved it. 'I can see you are, now.'

'The other one has gone. She won't be back.'

'Never.' John Welbeck's eyes were bright. 'I've found her. Stella.'

'But older.' She smiled at him. 'Free at last, John, but older.'

'Do I look as though I give a damn!'

They faced each other, and Kit suddenly saw old photographs come alive. A pretty girl and a gaunt young man. But Stella's hair was not so black as it had seemed. It may have been the grey light of the dawn, but Kit did not even want to know. She went forward and Stella stooped and kissed her.

Impulsively, John Welbeck had stepped forward and grasped Tekker's hand. 'All due to you, young man.' He still did not know Tekker's name. 'And the young lady.'

Tekker took his eyes from John Welbeck and looked beyond him to the plain where the grey mist made faint floating islands. 'But where is it?' he said. 'The palace? And the stairs?'

Stella was holding something towards him. He took the small disc of bog oak.

'You can still find it,' she said. 'Both of you. From time to time it will be there.'

And it was.